SCREAM FOR JEEVES

A Parody

SCREAM FOR JEEVES

A Parody

by

P. H. Cannon

author of *Pulptime*

illustrated by

J. C. Eckhardt

WODECRAFT PRESS

New York

For L. S.

This work is in no way authorized by the estates of P. G. Wodehouse, H. P. Love-craft, or Arthur Conan Doyle. It is purely a work of parody, and the fictional creations of these authors are used solely for the sake of humor.

Distributed by Necronomicon Press, 101 Lockwood St., West Warwick, RI 02893

Manufactured in U.S.A.

10 9 8 7 6 5 4 3 2

First Edition

ISBN 0-940-88461-5
    0-940-88460-7 [pbk.]

Contents

"There are, in fact, no ignorant aristocrats in Lovecraft--a reflexion, perhaps, of his wish to believe all aristocrats intelligent or, at the very least, supportive of intellectual effort."--S. T. JOSHI

"I am aware of a certain discomfort, emanating from the realization that all text is intertext--that stories do not have boundaries or edges that separate them from each other or from other texts, that they may even be spliced or woven together, if we wish."--DONALD R. BURLESON

CHAPTER 1

Cats, Rats, and Bertie Wooster

I AM AFRAID, Jeeves, that we shall have to go," I said, as I nipped into the eggs and b. late one bright summer morning.

"Go, sir? Pray may I ask where to, sir?"

"To Anchester--to Exham Priory."

The telegram that Jeeves had delivered with the breakfast tray had been a lulu, a *crie de coeur* from my old friend Captain Edward "Tubby" Norrys:

> *I say Bertie old man help. I am stuck here in this newly restored mediæval monstrosity trying to buck up this gloomy old American bird progenitor of my late comrade at arms Alf Melmoth Delapore. Pop Delapore or de la Poer as he now styles himself you know how these Americans like to affect ancestral spellings Bertie has been having dreams of the queerest sort. All the cats have been acting rum as well. Come here at once and bring Jeeves. Jeeves is the only one who can get to the bottom of this mystery Bertie.--TUBBY*

"What do you make of it, Jeeves?"

"Most sinister, sir."

"I know, Jeeves. Americans with sackfuls of the greenstuff to roll in tend to the eccentric. Throw in a few overexcited cats and you've got a recipe for disaster." As a rule I'm fond of the feline tribe, but in the aftermath of a certain luncheon engagement--of which more later--cats were for the moment low on my list.

"I would advocate the utmost caution in any effort to assist Captain Norrys, sir."

"But dash it all, Jeeves, Tubby and I were at school together. I suppose there's nothing for it. Telegraph the chump we're on our way, then crank up the two-seater. We leave in half-an-hour."

"Very good, sir."

I don't know whether you've travelled much in the remoter reaches of the Welsh border, but that is where Jeeves and I found ourselves at dusk that evening. First the deserted streets of a forgotten village, where Jeeves spoke of the Augustan Legion and the clash of arms, and all the tremendous pomp that followed the eagles; then the broad river swimming to full tide, the wide meadows, the cornfields whitening, and the deep lane winding on the slope between the hills and the water. At last we began to ascend and could see the half-shaped outlines of hills beyond, and in the distance the glare of the furnace fire on the precipice from whose brink Exham Priory overlooked a desolate valley three miles west of the village of Anchester.

"A lonely and curious country, Jeeves," I said, casting the eye at the great and ancient wood on either side of the road. It was not a sight to put one in the mood to pull over for a loaf of bread and a jug of wine, if you know what I mean.

"In the words of Machen, sir, 'A territory all strange and unvisited, and more unknown to Englishmen than the very heart of Africa.'"

"Machen?"

"Arthur Machen, sir."

The name was new to me. "Pal of yours?"

"Indeed, sir, the distinguished Welsh mystic and fantaisiste was a frequent visitor in my youth to my Aunt Purefoy's house in Carleon-on-Usk."

A short time later we turned into a drive and the towers of the priory, formerly part of the estate of the Norrys family, hove into view. The light was dim but I could not help thinking of that morbid American poet--the chappie who went about sozzled with a raven on his shoulder, don't you know, the one who penned those immortal lines:

> *Tum tum tum-tum tum tum tum-tum*
> *By good angels tum-tum-tum*
> *Tum tum tum tum stately palace--*
> *Tum-tum-tum palace--reared its head.*

"Quite the stately palace, er stately home, Jeeves, what?"

"Exham Priory is known for its peculiarly composite architecture, sir. Gothic towers rest on a Saxon or Romanesque substructure, whose foundation in turn is of a still earlier order or blend of orders--Roman, and even Druidic or native Cymric, if legends speak truly. Furthermore, sir, the priory stands on the site of a prehistoric temple; a Druidical or ante-Druidical thing which must have been contemporary with Stonehenge."

"Thank you, Jeeves." It beats me where Jeeves picks up this stuff, but the man is forever improving the mind by reading books of the highest brow.

We were greeted in the front hall by Tubby, who as he waddled across the marble more than ever resembled one of those Japanese Sumo wrestlers after an especially satisfying twelve-course meal--except in this case, of course, dinner had been held up pending our arrival.

"I'm so glad you and Jeeves are finally here, Bertie. I'm afraid Pop de la Poer has been suffering from increasingly severe delusions."

"Off his onion, is he?"

"You must jolly along the old boy as best you can, Bertie. Humour him in his every whim, until Jeeves can figure out what the devil is going on."

"You can count on Bertram to rally round and display the cheerful countenance," I assured the amiable fathead, who shook in gratitude like a jelly--or more precisely a pantry full of jellies.

A servant showed me to my room, a circular chamber in the east tower, where by the light of electric bulbs which rather clumsily counterfeited candles, I changed into evening clothes. Jeeves shimmered in as invisibly as the sheeted figure of ghostly lore and, as usual, assisted with the knotting of the tie.

"Mr. de la Poer's valet has just informed me of restlessness among all the cats in the house last night, sir."

"*All* the cats? Tell me, Jeeves, just how many of the bally creatures do you suppose infest this infernal shack?"

"Nine, sir. They were seen to rove from room to room, restless and disturbed, and to sniff constantly about the walls which form part of the old Gothic structure."

The subject of cats reminded me of the recent occasion on which Sir Roderick Glossup, the nerve specialist, came to lunch at my flat. Jeeves had fixed it so that the young master had appeared an absolute loony, one of his fruitier wheezes having been to stick an overripe salmon in the bedroom by an open window. No sooner had Sir Roderick and I slipped on the nose-bags than a frightful shindy had started from the next room, sounding as though all the cats in London, assisted by delegates from outlying suburbs, had got together to settle their differences once and for all. You can see why the prospect of a chorus of cats at Exham Priory did not appeal.

"When he reported the incident to his master, sir," continued Jeeves, "the man suggested that there must be some singular odour or emanation from the old stonework, imperceptible to human senses, but affecting the delicate organs of cats even through the new woodwork."

"Something smells fishy here, Jeeves," I said, still quaking from the memory of the remains I had found on the bedroom carpet after about a hundred and fifteen cats had finished their picnic.

"I suspect the source of this odour or emanation is a bird of an altogether different feather, sir, if you will pardon my saying so. In my estimation, the evidence indicates intramural murine activity."

"Rats in the walls, eh? Well, I'll give you odds on, Jeeves, that nine cats will make short work of any vermin that dares poke its whiskers into the cheese *chez* de la Poer."

"I would not wish to hazard a wager on the outcome, sir, until we have ascertained the exact nature of this rodent manifestation."

"Speaking of the Stilton, Jeeves, it's time I legged it for the trough."

"*A bon chat, bon rat,* sir."

I went down to the dining room, where seated at the head of the table was a cove of about sixty-five, an austere New England type about whom there still seemed to cling the greyness of Massachusetts business life.

"What ho, what ho, what ho!" I said, trying to strike the genial note.

My host, who had been sipping at the soup like some small animal, suspended the spoon just long enough to murmur a reply, as if to say the arrival of a Wooster at the watering-hole was to him a matter of little concern. As I took my place at his elbow, I surmised that the old buzzard was going to prove about as garrulous as "Silent" Cal Coolidge, soon to become the American president after that other bloke would so unexpectedly cash in the poker chips. Tubby was clearly too busy shoveling the feed down the pit to hold up his end of the bright and sparkling. So, after a few crisp remarks on the weather, I turned the conversation round to ancestors. You know how Americans like to burble on about their ancestors, especially when they have any worth the price of eggs, and Pop de la Poer did not disappoint.

"Do you realise, Mr. Wooster, that the fireside tales represent the de la Poers as a race of hereditary dæmons besides whom Gilles de Retz and the Marquis de Sade would seem the veriest tyros?"

"Retz and Sade," I replied with a knowing nod of the lemon. "Weren't they those two French johnnies who went sixteen rounds with no decision in '03?"

"Some of the worst characters married into the family. Lady Margaret Trevor from Cornwall, wife of Godfrey, the second son of the fifth baron, became a favourite bane of children all over the countryside, and the heroine of a particularly horrible old ballad not yet extinct near the Welsh border."

"A ballad? Not the one by chance that starts, 'There was a young lady from Dorset / Who couldn't unfasten her corset'? I forget the middle part, but it ends something like 'Whatever you do, my good man, don't force it.'"

"Preserved in balladry, too, though not illustrating the same point, is the hideous tale of Mary de la Poer, who shortly after her marriage to the Earl of Shrewsfield was killed by him and his mother, both of the slayers being absolved and blessed by the priest to whom they confessed what they dared not repeat to the world."

"Frightful dragon, was she? Sounds a bit like my Aunt Agatha."

When the geezer had exhausted the subject of his ancestors--and a rum lot they were too, all cultists and murderers and health-food fanatics, if you could credit the old legends--he filled me in on present family circs.

"Mr. Wooster, I am a retired manufacturer no longer young. Three years ago I lost my only son, Alfred, my motherless boy."

"But surely your son must have had aunts?"

"When he returned from the Great War a maimed invalid I thought of nothing but his care, even placing my business under the direction of partners."

"Great War? Cavaliers and Roundheads, what?"

He went on to describe the restoration of the priory--it had been a stupendous task, for the deserted pile had rather resembled the ruins of one's breakfast egg--until finally, after wiping the remnants of an indifferent pear *soufflé* from the chin, the last of the de la Poers announced that he was sleepy and we packed it in for the night.

I wish I could report that the chat over the breakfast table the next morning was all sunshine and mirth, but it was not.

"I trust you slept well, Mr. Wooster," said my host, as he pushed the kippers about the plate in a morose, devil-take-the-hindmost sort of way.

"Like a top, old sport. Like a top."

"I was harassec by dreams of the most horrible sort. First there was a vision of a Roman feast like hat of Trimalchio, with a horror in a covered platter."

"Could it have been something you ate?" I said, sounding the solicitious note. I didn't want to hurt the old fellow's feelings, of course, so I refrained from saying that the fish sauce the night before had been somewhat below par. In truth, the cook at Exham Priory was rot even in the running with Anatole, my Aunt Dahlia's French chef and God's gift to the gastric juices.

"Next I seemed to be looking down from an immense height upon a twilit grotto, knee-deep in filth, where a white-bearded dæmon swineherd drove about with his staff a flock of fungous, flabby beasts whose appearance filled me with unutterable loathing."

"Could it have been something you read before retiring? 'Mary Had a Little Lamb' perhaps? Mind you, that one's about a shepherdess, not a swineherd, but it's the same sort of thing, don't you know."

"Then, as the swineherd paused and nodded over his task, a mighty swarm of rats rained down on the stinking abyss and fell to devouring beasts and man alike."

"Rats! By Jove, this is getting a bit thick. My man Jeeves thinks rats may have been the party to blame for your cats carrying on the other day like they had broken into the catnip."

Well, this emulsion of cats and rats would soon get even thicker. Tubby and I spent an uneventful afternoon messing about the priory's extensive gardens, filled with coarse vegetables, which were to turn up at the evening meal as a sodden *mélange*. That night the pumpkin had barely hit the pillow of the four-poster before there arose a veritable nightmare of feline yelling and clawing from somewhere below. I put on the dressing gown and went out to investigate, finding a pyjama-clad Pop de la Poer in the midst of an army of cats running excitedly around the oak-panelled walls of the study.

"The walls are alive with nauseous sound--the verminous slithering of raven-ous, gigantic rats!" exclaimed the master of the manse.

"You don't say. As a child I think I read something about a giant rat of Suma-tra--or at any rate, a passing reference."

"You imbecile, can't you hear them stampeding in the walls?"

Before I could reply in the negative, the entire four-footed crew plunged pre-cipitously out the door, down several flights of stairs, beating us in the biped class by several lengths to the closed door of the sub-cellar. There the gang proceeded to squat, yowling. Shortly we were joined at the portal by Tubby, Jeeves, and a host of household servants, and after some floor debate the committee resolved to explore the sub-cellar while the trail was still hot, so to speak. As we descended, lantern in hand and the cats in the vanguard, we could not repress a thrill at the knowledge that the vault was built by Roman mittens.

"Every low arch and massive pillar is Roman, sir," observed Jeeves. "Not the debased Romanesque of the bungling Saxons, but the severe and harmonious classicism of the age of the Caesars."

"I say, Jeeves, take a gander at these inscriptions: P. GETAE ... TEMP ... DONA ... L. PRAEC ... VS ... PONTIFI ... ATYS .... Atys? Isn't he one of those chaps one reads in third-year Latin?"

"Atys is not an author, sir, but I have read Catullus and know something of the hideous rites of the Eastern god, whose worship was so mixed with that of Cybele."

"Catullus." The name had an ominous ring. "No connection with cats, I hope?"

"None, sir."

"Ah, that's a relief."

The dumb chums, if that's the term I want, had in fact ceased their howls and were licking their fur and otherwise behaving in a peaceful, law-abiding manner near a group of brown-stained blocks--or altars, according to Jeeves--except for one alabaster old gentleman, who was pawing frantically around the bottom of the large stone altar in the centre of the room.

"Hullo, what is it, Snow-Man?" asked Tubby. Like the proverbial mountain that toddled off to Mahomet, my friend rolled over to the altar in question and set down the lantern the better to scrape among the lichens clustered at the base. He did not find anything, and was about to abandon his efforts, when Jeeves coughed in that unobtrusive way of his, like a sheep clearing its throat in the mist.

"Pardon me, sir, but I think the company should note that the lantern is slightly but certainly flickering from a draught of air which it had not before received, and which comes indubitably from the crevice between floor and altar where Captain Norrys was scraping away the lichens."

"How right you are, Jeeves." We Woosters are renowned for our fighting ancestors--the grand old Sieur de Wocestre displayed a great deal of vim at the Battle of Agincourt--but there are times when it is prudent to blow the horn of alarm and execute a tactical withdrawal.

We spent the rest of the night in the brilliantly lighted study, wagging the chin over what we should do next. The discovery that some vault deeper than the deepest known masonry of the Romans underlay the sub-cellar had given us a nasty jar. Should we try to move the altar stone and risk landing in the soup below--or throw in the towel and wash our hands of it for good?

"Well, Jeeves," I said at last, after the rest of us had exercised the brain cells to no avail. "Do you have any ideas?"

"I would recommend that you compromise, sir, and return to London to gather a group of archæologists and scientific men fit to cope with the mystery."

"I say, that's a capital idea!" exclaimed Tubby. Even de la Poer *père* grumbled his assent, and everyone agreed that this was a masterly course of action, one that Napoleon would have been proud to hit upon in his prime.

"You stand alone, Jeeves," I said.

"I endeavour to give satisfaction, sir."

"Er ... any chance you might like to have a go at braving the unknown depths by yourself, Jeeves?"

"I would prefer not to, sir. *Nolle prosequi*."

"As you please, Jeeves."

"Thank you, sir."

Less than a fortnight later I was still congratulating myself upon my narrow escape from Castle de la Poer and its pestilential pets--I had begged off the subsequent recruitment drive and been lying low ever since--when Jeeves floated in and announced a visitor on the doorstep.

"Captain Norrys to see you, sir."

"Tubby, eh? Did he say what he wanted, Jeeves?"

"He did not confide his mission to me, sir."

"Very well, Jeeves," I said, hoping against hope that the poor sap wished to see me on some neutral affair, like our going partners in the forthcoming annual Drones Darts Tournament. "Show him in."

For a moment I thought a gelatin dessert of a size to gag an elephant had come to pay its respects--and spoil the sitting-room rug with its viscous trail--but it was, of course, only my roly-poly pal.

"Bertie, how are you?"

"Couldn't be better--now that I've returned to the metrop." I meant to sound cool and distant, but it did no good. The human pudding continued to wax enthusiastic.

"Bertie, you must come back to Exham Priory to explore the sub-sub-cellar with us. It'll be such a lark."

"Tubby, I'd sooner saunter down the aisle with Honoria Glossup than go back to that dungeon." In case I didn't mention it, la Glossup is Sir R.'s daughter, a dreadful girl who forced me to read Nietzsche during the brief period of our engagement. Or am I confusing her with Florence Craye, another horror who once viewed Bertram as ripe for reform through matrimony?

"Please, Bertie. We've rounded up some prize scientific chaps, five real corkers, including Sir William Brinton."

"Sir William who?"

"As I recall, sir," said Jeeves from the sideboard, "Sir William's excavations in the Troad excited most of the world in their day."

"Thank you, Jeeves, but this egghead's credentials are not--what's the word I want, Jeeves?"

"Germane, sir?"

"Yes--they are not germane to the issue. For another thing, I have the distinct feeling I've worn out the welcome mat in this de la Poer's baleful eyes. For all my lending of the sympathetic ear and shoulder, ours was hardly a teary farewell."

"I'm not asking much, Bertie."

"What would you have me do next, Tubby, pinch the old blister's favourite cat?"

"Bertie, we were at school together."

Well, what could I do? In the final appeal a Wooster always rallies round his old schoolmates. One must obey the Code.

"All right then, I'll go."

"Stout fellow, Bertie. Oh, and be sure you bring Jeeves. While these scientific chappies may be brainy enough in their own fields, no one beats Jeeves in the over-all grey-matter department."

It may in fact have been a sign of his high intelligence that Jeeves was not particularly keen on the idea of a return engagement at Exham Priory, but in the end he dutifully accompanied the young master for an encore performance. All was tranquil late that August morning when we gathered in the sub-cellar. The cast included nine members of the human species and one of the feline, for the investigators were anxious that Snow-Man be present in case any rats, living or spectral, tried to give us the raspberry. While Sir William Brinton, discreetly assisted by Jeeves, directed the raising of the central altar stone, I chatted with one of the assembled savants, a fellow named Thornton, devoted to the psychic.

"Any notions what might lie in store below?" I asked, thinking he might have more insight than those with a more materialist bent.

"Matter is as really awful and unknown as spirit," the man explained in a tone that suggested it all should be perfectly plain to a child. "Science itself but dallies on the threshold, scarcely gaining more than a glimpse of the wonders of the inner place."

"Yes, quite. I see what you mean," I replied, though frankly I didn't.

Within an hour the altar stone was tilting backwards, counterbalanced by Tubby, and there lay revealed-- But how shall I describe it? I don't know if you've ridden much through the tunnel-of-horrors featured at the better amusement parks, but the scene before us reminded me strongly of same. Through a nearly square opening in the tiled floor, sprawling on a flight of stone steps, was a ghastly array of human or semi-human bones. Not a pretty sight, you understand, but at least there was a cool breeze with something of freshness in it blowing up the arched passage. I mean to say, it could have been a noxious rush as from a closed vault. We did not pause long, but shiveringly began to cut a swath through the ancestral debris down the steps. It was then that Jeeves noticed something odd.

"You will observe, sir, that the hewn walls of the passage, according to the direction of the strokes, must have been chiselled from beneath."

"*From beneath* you say, Jeeves?"

"Yes, sir."

"But in that case--"

"For the sake of your sanity, sir, I would advise you not to ruminate on the implications."

I wonder that any man among us wasn't sticking straws in his hair ere long, for at the foot of the steps we stumbled into a twilit grotto of enormous height that in atmosphere rivalled the scalier London nightclubs in the wee hours.

"Great Scott!" I cried.

"My God!" croaked another throat.

Tubby in his inarticulate way merely gargled, while Jeeves raised his left eyebrow a quarter of an inch, a sure sign of emotional distress.

There were low buildings that I imagine even Noah would have considered shabby with age--and bones heaped about everywhere, as if someone intent on emptying the closet of the family skeleton had instead uprooted the entire family tree. After recovering from the initial shock, the others set about examining the dump, no doubt a fascinating process if you were an anthropologist or an architect--but not so to Bertram, whose nerve endings by this time were standing an inch out from the skin. I had just lit up a calming gasper, when that fiend Snow-Man, taking offence perhaps at the sudden flare of the match, pounced out of the shadows toward the trouser leg. My nerves shot out another inch, and for the nonce panic overthrew sweet reason in the old bean. I fled headlong into the midnight cavern, with the hellcat in hot pursuit.

I gave the blasted animal the slip in the dark but, dash it, I eventually realised I'd lost the human herd.

"I say there, Tubby, where are you?" I hollered. "Jeeves, I say, hall-o, hall-o, hall-o!"

Well, I kept wandering about and calling, don't you know, and thinking how tiresome it was to play blind-man's-bluff for one. Then something bumped into me--something hard and lean. I knew it wasn't rats--though in a manner of speaking, I imagine you could say it was one big rat. I instantly recognised the American accent: "Shall a Wooster hold the hand of a de la Poer? ... He's cuckoo, I tell you...that spineless worm... Curse you, Wooster, I'll teach you to goggle at what my family do!" Further aspersions on the Wooster name followed, some in Latin, a language I rather enjoy hearing, especially from Jeeves, but not in present circs. When the blighter began to growl like a pagan lion in search of its next Christian, I decided it was high time to hoof it. It wasn't a graceful exit. I scampered off and was cruising at about forty m.p.h. when I rammed the coco-nut against an object even harder on

Mohs' scale than Pop de la Poer--or so it felt in that final moment before everything went black.

After what seemed like æons, I awoke to find myself home in bed, the melon throbbing. I was just about to ring for Jeeves, when the faithful servitor drifted in with the tissue-restorer on the salver.

"Good Lord! Was it Boat-Race Night last night?" Then I quaffed the soothing brew, and our underground adventure all came back to me like a pulp thriller.

"What happened, Jeeves?" I groaned.

"After three hours we discovered you in the blackness, sir. It appears that you collided with a low-hanging rock. You will be relieved to learn that the physicians anticipate a full recovery."

"Venture far into that grisly Tartarus, did you?"

"We shall never know what sightless Stygian worlds yawn beyond the little distance we went, sir, for it was decided that such secrets are not good for mankind."

"Quite the wisest course, Jeeves, if you ask me. Man has done jolly well to date without shining the spotlight at the dirt under the carpet at Exham Priory, and I daresay if he keeps a lid on it for the future he'll be all right."

"*Dulce est ignorantia*, sir."

Despite his assurances, however, I could see by a faint twitching of the lip that Jeeves was troubled.

"Do you have something unpleasant to tell me, Jeeves?"

"Yes, sir. Unfortunately, I have some extremely disturbing news to impart."

"Out with it then, my man. Don't brood."

"I regret that it is my mournful duty to inform you, sir, that certain members of our subterranean expedition suffered grave harm." The lip again wavered. "Mr. de la Poer..."

"Gone totally potty, has he?"

"It is my understanding of his case that his aberration has grown from a mere eccentricity to a dark mania, involving a profound and peculiar personality change. Reversion to type, I believe, is the term employed by the professional psychologists. Mr. de la Poer is presently ensconced at Hanwell Hospital, under the direct supervision of Sir Roderick Glossup."

"Takes a loony to cure a loony, I always say."

"As for Captain Norrys, sir..." Jeeves coughed, like a sheep choking on a haggis. "An accident befell him that resulted in massive and irreversible physical trauma."

"You mean to say, Jeeves, he's handed in the dinner-pail?"

"Yes, sir. If I may say so, the manner of his passing was exceedingly gruesome."

"Spare me the details, Jeeves." I laughed. One of those short bitter ones.

"It would seem that Providence doesn't always look after the chumps of this world," I said, after some sober reflection.

"Indeed not, sir."

"And now I'm faced with having to scare up a new partner for the Drones Darts Tournament, what?"

"Yes, sir."

"Any ideas?"

"As the matter does not require immediate attention, sir, I suggest you devote yourself to gaining further repose."

"Right then, Jeeves, I'll catch a spot more of the dreamless."

"Most sensible, sir. So soon after your ordeal you should take care to avoid passing beyond the Gate of Deeper Slumber into dreamland."

CHAPTER 2

Something Foetid

Y OU ASK me to explain why I don't go in for locking self in meat lockers overnight or joining expeditions to the South Pole. As those who know Bertram best will tell you, we Woosters prefer sunny skies and balmy breezes to blinding blizzards, hot water to ice in the bedroom. More fond of fair weather than of foul, of the cup of hot tea than of the flask of liquid nitrogen, I rarely catch cold. A nasty case, however, did keep me in bed during the two days of my betrothal to Pauline Stoker. What I will do is to relate the circs., and leave it to you to judge whether or not the young master acted like an absolute ass.

Soon after recovering from the rummy affair of the cats and rats and atavistic urges run amok which my late chum Captain Edward "Tubby" Norrys got me mixed up in, I decided it would be a sound scheme to settle down for a spell of exile in the city of New York. I know some chaps think that New York is not a sentient perpetuation of Old New York as the metrop. is of Old London and Gay Parée of Old Paris; that it is in fact dead as a dormouse and its denizens all mad as hatters. But, dash it, I'm bound to say New York's a most sprightly place to be exiled in. Everybody was awfully good to me; blokes introduced me to other blokes, and it wasn't long before I knew squads of the right sort--artists and writers and so forth.

Randy, the bird I am about to treat of, was one of the writers. He told me at our first meeting that he had once been an author of popular novels: "They were very graceful novels, in which I mirthlessly and urbanely laughed at the dreams I lightly sketched; but I saw that their sophistication had sapped all their life away. Ironic humour dragged down all the twilight minarets I reared, and the earthly fear of improbability blasted all the delicate and amazing flowers in the færy gardens."

"Fairies in the garden, you say. Have you by chance been to Cottingley? Conan Doyle in that recent book of his reports that the place is swarming with the tiny wingèd creatures. He's got the snapshots to prove it, too."

Over the past couple of years Randy had turned his quill to another literary form, the short story. One of his efforts, he said with some pride, had had an unexpected effect upon the public: "When my tale, 'The Attic Window,' appeared in the January, 1922, issue of *Whispers*, in a good many places it was taken off the stands at the complaints of silly milksops."

"I had a piece, 'What the Well-dressed Young Man is Wearing,' in *Milady's Boudoir*, my Aunt Dahlia's magazine," I replied, not to be outdone. "Though I must say it didn't create the same kind of frenzy among the milque-toasts."

Whatever the aesthetic rewards of this market, the financial ones had been nothing to write home about. In the spring of 1923 Randy had to secure some dreary and unprofitable magazine work; and being unable to pay any substantial rent, began drifting from one cheap boarding establishment to another until coming upon a house in West Fourteenth Street which gave him the pip rather less than the others he had sampled. The floors were clean, the linen tolerably regular, the hot water not too often cold or turned off; and although the inhabitants were mostly Spaniards of the wrong sort, there was one inmate that you wouldn't be ashamed to take to your club, a doctor by the name of Muñoz. This Muñoz, unfortunately, couldn't even accept an invitation out to the corner chemist, as he suffered from some queer ailment that confined him to his flat.

For my friend this invalid's welfare had of late become an *idée fixe*, if that's the term I want, so when Randy trickled into my apartment one forenoon, I knew his visit had to concern his fellow-lodger. The very first words I spoke were: "Randy, how is Doc Muñoz?"

The poor chap gave one of those mirthless and urbane laughs. He was looking anxious and worried, like a fairy who has flitted too long amidst twilight minarets and amazing flowers.

"I'm so scared, Bertie," said Randy. "Hector's too sick to look after himself-- he's sicker and sicker all the time. He relies on the landlady's son to bring him food and laundry and medicines and chemicals. Not only that, he does all his own housework."

"Does all his own housework! Great Scott, the queasy blighter must be at the end of his bally tether. Is there nothing to be done?"

"Bertie, that's why I stopped by today. Though Hector refuses to consult a doctor, I'm sure he'd welcome a visit from someone with a mind as keen and analytical as a physician's, someone who understands the psychology of the individual, someone--"

"My blushes, Randy," I murmured in a deprecating voice.

"--someone, in short, like your man Jeeves."

About my man Jeeves, I mean to say, what? I'll be the first to admit that from the collar upward he stands alone. But, dash it, he's not the only member of the Wooster household who can lend the glad hand in time of need. I was just about to issue a snappy rejoinder, when the man himself shimmered in, his map as blank as a night-gaunt's. Stifling my pique, I put the facts of the case before him and asked if he would delve into the matter.

"I have nothing to suggest at present, sir."

"Nothing, Jeeves?"

"Nothing, sir."

From a certain frostiness in Jeeves's tone, I deduced that something was amiss. Then it struck me: the fellow was still sulking over the patterned suit I had picked up for a mere twenty dollars the other day in Brooklyn and was even now sporting on the person.

"Jeeves objects to my new suit, Randy, but I tell you, a chappie can't go wrong at Franklin Clothes."

"An headquarters of prize-fight hangers-on and race-track touts, if you will pardon my saying so, sir."

"It's a pity, Jeeves, that you fail to appreciate the fizziest and freshest in American men's fashion. Wouldn't you agree, Randy?"

"Well, Bertie, let me put it this way. If I were you I'd steer clear of Italian restaurants. In those duds you might be mistaken for a tablecloth."

In the end I ventured downtown alone that evening to Randy's place on West Fourteenth Street, a four-story mansion of brownstone, oldish by American standards, and fitted with woodwork and marble that looked as if they had been salvaged from the Augean stables--before Hercules applied the mop and broom. I was met in the hall by the landlady, Mrs. Herrero, whose whiskered mug would have qualified her as the star attraction of any circus sideshow.

"Ah, Mistair Jeeves. I so glad you come."

"Wooster's the name, my good man ... er, woman."

"Is just in time. Doctair Muñoz, he have speel his chemicals."

"Well, I shouldn't worry if he spilled his chemicals on the woodwork or marble. I daresay no one will notice."

"All day he take funnee-smelling baths."

"Oh, really? Perhaps he got soap in his eyes and grabbed the jar of hydrogen sulfide instead of the bubble-bath."

"He cannot get excite."

"He can't get outside? Yes, I know, Randy told me, but--"

"And the sal-ammoniac--"

"Sal who?"

"*Qué?*"

I was prepared to play Pat to Mrs. Herrero's Mike as long as I had to, but at that moment Randy arrived and put the kibosh on the cross-talk. "Don't mind her," he explained, as he clouted his landlady affectionately on the occiput, "she's from Barcelona."

"He great once," Mrs. Herrero cried after us, as we tripped up the stairs. "My faither in Barcelona have hear of heem."

Doc Muñoz lived on the top floor, directly above Randy, in a bedsitter suite complete with laboratory. Our knock on the door was answered by a pint-size bloke who looked about as lifelike as one of those waxworks at Madame Tussaud's. A puss as livid as a plum pie was adorned with a short iron-grey beard, somewhat less full than the chin-fungus on Mrs. Herrero.

"I've brought someone to see you, Hector," said my companion.

"I told you no visitors, Randy," the man--or mannikin--replied in a voice that sounded like a gramophone record after about the two-thousandth play. It was hard to believe that this gargoyle had once impressed the lower orders of Barcelona with his greatness.

"Mr. Wooster here's no ordinary visitor, Hector. He's, uh ... he's uh, had a heartattack and in need of medical attention," my pal improvised. The doc remained unmoved--and unmoving--like a stuffed baboon. "Please, Hector, let us in. Last week you fixed the arm of that mechanic--O'Reilly, wasn't it?--who got hurt all of a sudden."

"Very well, enter," he rasped.

"How kind of you. It's nothing really--just a wee twinge of the aortic valve," I said, warming to my *role*, though it didn't stay warm for long. As we crossed the threshold, we were struck by a blast of chill air that would have staggered Scott of the Antarctic. Refrigerating machinery resembling some futurist's nightmare and rumbling like a locomotive filled up about half the room--which smelled like a perfume emporium of the sort patronised by the cheaper class of shopgirl.

"I have a fondness for exotic spices and Egyptian incense," our host confided.

You might not have trusted Doc Muñoz to judge the roses at your garden-club flower show, but in another department he displayed superior blood and breeding.

"I greatly admire your suit, Mr. Wooster," he said, as I removed the collar and shirt studs. "The cut and fit are perfect."

"Would that everyone were as discriminating," I replied, throwing Randy a meaningful glance.

In the course of the examination, the doc explained his methods: "I am the bitterest of sworn enemies to death, Mr. Wooster, and have sunk my fortune and lost all my friends in a lifetime of bizarre experiments devoted to its bafflement and extirpation."

"Oh, yes?"

"I do not scorn the incantations of the mediævalists, since I believe these cryptic formulae to contain rare psychological stimuli which might conceivably have singular effects on the substance of a nervous system from which all organic pulsations have fled."

"Ah."

"Will and consciousness are stronger than organic life itself, so that if a bodily frame be but originally healthy and carefully preserved, it may through a scientific enhancement of these qualities retain a kind of nervous animation despite the most serious impairments, defects, or even absences in the battery of specific organs."

"!?"

No doubt Jeeves could have put a finger on the nub of this bedside banter, but it was all Greek to Bertram, who by this juncture was quivering like an aspen, what with frost forming on the exposed anatomy and *eau de shopgirl* running riot through the nasal passages.

After pronouncing the core of the Wooster corpus brim full of organic pulsations, the doc proceeded to gas about an aged sawbones of his acquaintance, one Torres of Valencia, who had shared his earlier experiments and nursed him through a great illness some eighteen years before: "No sooner had the venerable practitioner saved me than he himself succumbed to the grim enemy he had fought.

Perhaps the strain had been too great, for the methods of healing had been most extraordinary, involving scenes and processes not welcomed by elderly and con-servative Galens."

"I say, old top,' I replied. "Sounds as if this Torres would have been better off shoving his scenes and processes at the more youthful and liberal natives of Galencia."

After some further cheery chit-chat about the good old days back in Iberia, Randy and I made out exit. Our departure came none too soon for Wooster, B. It's one thing to brave the hazardous elements and odours of a stranger's apartment but quite another to have to hold up your end of the bright and sparkling with a being who oozes the kind of charm and vitality one usually associates with a ventrilo-quist's dummy.

At the front door my friend expressed his disappointment that our party had been short one member: "I'm sorry you couldn't persuade Jeeves to join us, Bertie. However, maybe Jeeves can figure out how to help Hector when you report to him."

"*If* I report to him," I shot back. And I meant it to sting.

Back home, after a hot bath free of all funny smells, I of course felt much chirpier. When Jeeves drifted in with the nightcap on the salver, I gave him the low-down on the evening's adventure with a blithe spirit: "So there you have it, Jeeves. Doc Muñoz has an excellent eye for fashion, but over the years these queer medical experiments have left him a spent force."

"Most eldritch, sir."

"Quite, Jeeves."

"If I may be permitted to say so, sir, Dr. Muñoz's ideas appear to be as funda-mentally unsound as those of Nietzsche."

"You're entitled to your opinion, Jeeves, though Randy assures me other-wise." My literary chum had once shown me a piece in one of those obscure journals he contributes to--"Nietzcheism [sic] and Idealism" I think was the title--which suggested that the ideas of this self-styled superman were sound as a bell.

"I would not rely on Mr. Carter's judgement, sir."

"Why not, Jeeves?" I replied a trifle testily. "Why shouldn't I put complete faith in the judgement of one who has sacrificed all for Art?"

"I have made inquiries in your absence, sir. His assertions to the contrary, Mr. Carter does not depend solely on story sales to the pulp magazines for his livelihood."

"Oh, no?"

"No, sir. In truth, the gentleman is a millionaire of extremely eccentric tastes and habits. His slumming in New York City, sir, is but his latest fancy."

"Who fed you this folderol, Jeeves?"

"His man Parks, sir. He was kind enough to supply the essential background information."

"His man Parks?"

"Yes, sir. Parks looks after a second residence that Mr. Carter clandestinely maintains in a far more suitable neighbourhood of the city than the one he ostensibly calls home."

One does not as a rule enjoy one's valet accusing one's friends of playing false, and now was no exception. "Randy comes of an ancient line, Jeeves, composed of delicate and sensitive men with strange visions," I said hotly.

"Indeed, sir."

"A flame-eyed Crusader learnt wild secrets of the Saracens that held him captive."

"Very good, sir."

"The first Sir Randolph Carter studied magic when Elizabeth was queen."

"Yes, sir."

"And Edmund Carter just escaped hanging in the Salem witchcraft."

"*Quod erat demonstratum*, sir. I fear Mr. Carter has inherited the family predilection for the *outré*. Parks informs me that Mr. Carter once lived with a man in the south and shared his studies for seven years, till horror overtook them one midnight in an unknown and archaic graveyard, and only one emerged where two had entered."

"Sheer rot, Jeeves."

"Parks for years has born patiently with his master's vagaries, sir."

"What utter tripe."

"I would advise you, sir, not to allow Mr. Carter to draw you any deeper into this matter concerning Dr. Muñoz. It is apparent that Dr. Muñoz is beyond all earthly assistance. As the lesser of two evils, sir, I recommend that you accept the invitation which Miss Pauline Stoker issued over the 'phone this evening. Miss Stoker desires you to visit her at her father's Long Island estate at your earliest convenience."

I paused, taking a pensive sip from the beaker. I was dashed if I would humble myself before the man, yet perhaps Jeeves did smell a genuine stinker. There was something foetid about this Muñoz business. Although Pauline Stoker is one of those hearty girls who insists on playing five sets of tennis before breakfast, her taste in perfume is above reproach.

"Right you are, Jeeves. A spot of fresh country air would do wonders for the old aortic valve."

"Very good, sir."

"Oh, and Jeeves," I said, as if the idea were merely a careless afterthought. "When you pack my bag, please be sure to include my new suit, the one from Franklin Clothes."

"Surely not, sir," said Jeeves in a low, cold voice, as if he had been bitten on the leg by a zoog.

I could see that I was in for yet another round in that colossal contest of wills which from time to time darkens our relationship. But, fortified by the soothing beverage, I stood my ground. After a good deal of give-and-take we reached a split decision: the garment in question would travel with me to the country--but not Jeeves.

"I do not wish to be placed in a position, sir," the man protested, "where persons of refinement might misapprehend that I condone your wearing in public such Byzantine refuse."

As things turned out, I had no occasion to show off my new suit, as I spent most of my time *chez* Stoker recovering from a cold which no doubt had originated within the polar precincts of Doc Muñoz's bedsitter. Of course, the thirty-six holes of golf Pauline dragged me through the day I arrived--one of those crisp autumn days where the wind sweeps down the fairway in frore gusts as if from interstellar space--may have further weakened the Wooster constitution. Or then again it may have been the proposal of marriage I let slip in a moment of madness after sinking a fifteen-footer on the seventeenth. Whatever the source of my affliction, I stayed in bed for forty-eight hours, dosed with three different nostrums. The third night I had just begun to descend the seven hundred steps to the Gate of Deeper Slumber, when a servant awoke me with an urgent summons to the 'phone.

"Bertie!" gasped a familiar voice over the line. "Thank heavens I've reached you. The pump on Hector's refrigerating machine has broken down. Within three hours the process of ammonia cooling will become impossible. You must return to the city at once."

"But I say, Randy, it's past eleven o'clock and I'm feeling far from perky."

"I've checked the train schedule, Bertie. You'll have plenty of time to catch the 12:03 back to town."

"Why don't you ring up, Jeeves?"

"Jeeves was over earlier this evening--he gave me your number in the country--but damn the luck, he seems to have gone off for the night. I get no answer at your apartment. Not only that, I can't reach my man Parks."

"You never told me you employed a man, Randy."

"No, Bertie, I guess I never did."

"You know, Randy, Jeeves has told me some rum stories about your past."

For a few seconds all I could hear in the receiver was a kind of guttural coughing, like a ghast choking on a gug.

"Sorry, Bertie. I know at times I haven't been totally on the level," my friend conceded. "Still, I have always tried to live as befits a man of keen thought and good heritage."

"Would you say, Randy, that deserting a pal in an unknown and archaic graveyard at midnight befits a man of keen thought and good heritage?"

"I can explain, Bertie--"

"You shared a study with the chap for seven years!"

"Only five years--"

"I bet you were prefects together, too."

"Bertie, listen, uh… That night in the graveyard was, uh … was, uh, a school prank. Harley Warren came back from below. He was no fool… And this is no prank! This is an emergency, a matter of life and death!"

Well, what was a fellow to do in the face of such a piteous plea? I could not leave my chum in the lurch. Even on his bed of pain, a Wooster rallies round.

"Oh, very well then, Randy. I'll be there in a jiffy."

What with the train halting at every milk stop en route, and the dearth of cabs at the terminal in the wee hours, it was rather longer than a jiffy before I alighted at Randy's boarding-house. A sleepy and unshaven Mrs. Herrero greeted me at the door with a few choice epithets in her native tongue. Upstairs in the doc's flat I found Randy and the moribund hermit, the melon tightly bandaged, looking like a refugee from King Tut's tomb. The place no longer sounded like a locomotive at full throttle, and the pervading scent was now that of ammonia, redolent of the detergent Mrs. Herrero should have been using to swab down the woodwork and marble.

"Bertie! At last!" exclaimed my pal. A low rattle--one of those short hollow ones--issued from the throat of the mummy impersonator at his side.

"Were you by chance able to fix the fridge on your own, Randy?" I asked hopefully.

"I brought in O'Reilly from the neighbouring all-night garage, but he said nothing could be done till morning, when we'll have to get our hands on a new piston."

"Anything I can do?"

"Yes, as a matter of fact there is, Bertie. While I look after Hector here, please go out and get all the ice you can from every all-night drug store and cafeteria you can find. Okay?"

The prospect of traipsing about lower Manhattan before dawn, further risking the organic pulsations, did not appeal. Nonetheless, I spent the next couple of hours at the task, laying the spoils in front of the closed bathroom door, behind which the doc retired at about 5 a.m. "More--more!" the blister kept croaking, like a brat whose appetite for frozen treats knows no bounds.

At length a warmish day broke, and the shops opened one by one. It was then that Randy insisted I try to enlist the services of Mrs. Herrero's offspring, Esteban.

"Now see here, laddie," I said, holding up the defective part. "This pump piston."

"*Si.*"

"This ice." I gestured at the miniature igloo that now blocked the bathroom door.

"*Si.*"

"It's very simple. Either you go fetch the ice--or you order a new piston."

"How I order piston?"

"All right then, I'll order the piston and you fetch ice."

"*Qué?*"

A bop on the bean with the pump piston did not raise the level of the fathead's wits, though it did succeed in provoking the ire of Herrero *mère*, who was hovering in the vicinity like a mother hydra: "Mistair Woostair, I sorry. Esteban he can no help. No way, nossir."

Herrero and son slipped out through the puddles that for the nonce gave Doc Muñoz's bedsitter the appearance of an Arctic lagoon.

"That settles it," said Randy, raging violently. "Our only hope is to get ahold of Jeeves. You've got to give him another ring, Bertie."

We had been trying in vain every half-hour or so to telephone Jeeves and Parks at their respective digs, but only now, with the sun already high in the heavens, did I get through to the man.

"Jeeves, where have you been all night?" I said sharply.

"After looking in on Mr. Carter and Dr. Muñoz, sir, I joined Parks at his club, the New York branch of the Junior Ganymede. The amenities of that estimable institution proved so agreeable that we remained on the premises until eight o'clock this morning."

"Jeeves, I have been back in the burg since 3 a.m. and require your aid instanter."

"I apologise, sir. In view of the worrisome state of your health, I did not anticipate your returning quite so soon from the country. How may I be of assistance?"

I proceeded to outline the present crisis, drawing his attention to the crucial role of the pump piston.

"I had the opportunity to inspect the mechanism of which you speak last evening, sir. I believe I know of a suitable supply house far downtown where one might obtain a replacement. If you, sir, will perform this errand of mercy, Parks and I will meet you at Mr. Carter's West Fourteenth Street address with the appropriate tools for repair."

"Very good, Jeeves. We'll save the old doc yet!"

Well, what with discovering that Jeeves was wrong about the supply house he named and having to run hither and thither by subway and surface car to a number of other pump-piston purveyors, I did not return with the necessary part until approximately 1:30 p.m. By this time Bertram was a spent force and could barely drag self upstairs. In the hall outside the doc's apartment stood Jeeves, Randy, and a brisk little Cockney who could only have been Parks. Parks was busily chiding his master for allowing Doc Muñoz to shut them out: "Oy, guv'nor, so you leaves 'ome for ice and 'e in there sneaks out the bath and locks the bloomin' door, wot?" Jeeves was fiddling with some wire device at the door, behind which came no sound save a nameless sort of slow, thick dripping.

"Oh, Bertie," moaned my friend. "What kept you!"

"Dash it all, Randy, I did all I could!"

"I am afraid, sir, that you are not in time," said Jeeves solemnly.

"Not in time! You mean to say that my superhuman exertions over the past fourteen hours have been for naught? I spend half the night in a breathless, foodless search for ice and the whole morning in a hectic quest for pistons, and you tell me, Jeeves, you tell me I'm not in time?"

"It is most unfortunate, sir, but yes, that is the case."

I was sorely tempted to start smacking the lemon with the object of my wasted efforts, when Jeeves raised a restraining hand.

"I have just now managed to turn the key, sir," the man said coolly. "In your overexcited condition, sir, I would advise you to wait in the hall. Anyone else who chooses to enter should take the precaution of holding a pocket handkerchief to his nose."

Jeeves was referring to the nauseous odour that was seeping in waves from beneath the closed door, a fragrance rather reminiscent of the overripe salmon he once stuck in the bedroom while I lunched with my nemesis, the nerve specialist Sir Roderick Glossup. As the door swung open, revealing a south room blazing with the warm sun of early afternoon, the fishy smell swelled a thousandfold. The stomach churned, the knees buckled. The autumn heat lingered fearsomely. Then everything went black.

By the end of the week, after a programme featuring a thirty-six hour snooze followed by a steady diet of Jeeves's tissue-restorers, I had regained my pep.

Randy, on the other hand, when he came by, looked rather the worse for wear--like a fairy who has flitted so long amidst twilight minarets and amazing flowers that he has decided to call it a day and throw in the towel.

"I'm terribly sorry about Doc Muñoz, Randy," I said, offering my condolences. "But at least we gave it the old school try, what?"

"I guess so," the chump replied mournfully.

"Tut-tut, old stick. This Muñoz was scarcely the last word in loony old scholars. You'll soon find yourself another."

"I doubt it," sighed my friend. "By the way, Bertie, speaking of old scholars, I dreamed of my grandfather last night. He reminded me of a key..." Randy went on to describe a great silver key handed down from the Carters who consorted with wild-eyed Saracens and witches and what not. Housed in a carved oak box of archaic wonder, this key lay forgotten in the attic of the ancestral homestead in Arkham, Mass., whither the dreamer intended shortly to return.

"Hunting up old keys," I replied warmly. "Now there's a hobby not likely to land a chap in the soup, Randy."

After some final reflections on the occasionally titanic significance of dreams, my chum announced his departure: "So, Bertie, this is good-bye. Parks and I leave New York tomorrow."

Before I could return the farewell, Jeeves wafted in, smiling faintly, like an obliging ghoul.

"Good-bye, Jeeves," said Randy, turning to the man. "And thanks again for your gift. Hector would have approved."

"Thank you, sir."

"I say, Randy, what--" But the chap had already biffed off.

"Forgive me for interrupting, sir, but while you were entertaining Mr. Carter, Miss Pauline Stoker 'phoned."

"Oh?" I quavered. In all the recent excitement the bally girl had totally slipped my mind, and I dreaded hearing the sequel.

"Miss Stoker asked me to inform you, sir, that you may consider your engagement off as of the moment you sneaked out of her father's house."

"She's handing me the mitten, you say, Jeeves?"

"Your precipitous midnight flight did not impress her favourably--nor did your subsequent lack of communication, sir."

"You didn't explain I was busy helping a pal?"

"No, sir. I thought it best not to correct her negative view of your behaviour. Indeed, she was almost inclined to forgive you, except that--"

"Except what, Jeeves?"

"Except that Sir Roderick Glossup happened to have a word with her father, J. Washburn Stoker, about your past, sir."

Ever since the episode of the cats and the fish in the bedroom alluded to elsewhere in these memoirs of mine, R. Glossup has regarded Bertram as barmy to the core. While I wasn't privy to their colloquoy, of course, I've no doubt the old pot of poison convinced Pop Stoker to be wary of any prospective son-in-law who keeps a hundred and fifteen cats in the home.

"Well, Jeeves, if Randy can endure the demise of the doc," I said after musing awhile, "I suppose I can bear the loss of a fiancée." In all honesty it was a relief to realise I didn't have to order the new sponge-bag trousers and gardenia, because my nomination had been cancelled. Pauline's beauty had maddened me like wine, but even the finest vintages can leave a chap feeling fried.

"I am pleased to hear you express such a philosophical view of the situation, sir. If I might make a small confession--" Jeeves coughed.

"Yes, Jeeves?'

"I believe you would agree, sir, that Mr. Carter's concern for his upstairs neighbour had its peculiar aspects."

"Now that you mention it, Jeeves, Randy did overdo it a bit."

"Although Dr Muñoz was headed for a certain and familiar doom, sir, Parks and I resolved during your absence from the city to tip Nature's own sweet and cunning hand."

"What are you driving at, Jeeves?"

"I devised a strategem, sir, whereby I made an appointment to meet Dr. Muñoz. Parks and Mr. Carter were also present. At one point in the evening, while Parks distracted our hosts with an amusing imitation of their landlady, I took the opportunity to tinker with the pumping action of the refrigerating equipment."

"You mean to say, Jeeves, you bunged a monkey wrench into the machinery?"

"In effect, sir. Thereafter it was a simple matter, as you know--" Jeeves coughed again. "It was a simple matter to ensure that the pump was not repaired in time."

"Jeeves! Have you no shame?" I cried. It is one thing to admit to adding insult to injury, quite another to engage in conduct to which even a Machiavelli or a Borgia would hesitate to stoop.

"I can assure you, sir, that Parks and I acted in the best interest of his master. As for Dr. Muñoz--"

"I say, Jeeves, what about Doc Muñoz? What-in-the-devil did you find in the old bird's flat after my collapse?"

"Are you by chance familiar, sir, with Arthur Machen's 'Novel of the White Powder'?"

"Really, Jeeves. You should know the only novels I read are mysteries and thrillers. Cosmetics aren't in my line... Machen. Say, isn't he that pal of yours?"

"Yes, sir. The Welsh mystic used often to visit my Aunt Purefoy--"

"Oh, right, now I remember--you told me before. But I'm still in the dark about the doc."

"Very well, sir, do you recall the story by Edgar Allan Poe entitled 'Facts in the Case of M. Valdemar'?"

"That dimly rings a bell, Jeeves. Something about a little Frenchman who wears his arm in a sling, what?"

"Not exactly, sir."

"Oh, well, nevermind then... Oh, one last thing, Jeeves. That gift Randy was thanking you for. Dare I ask--"

"The gentleman was thanking me for your suit, sir."

"You don't mean my suit from Franklin Clothes, do you?"

"Yes, sir, I do. When I unpacked your bag after your return from Long Island, I took the liberty of notifying Mr. Carter of its availability."

"I can't imagine why Randy would want my suit, Jeeves."

"If I may explain, sir, the suit was not for the gentleman himself but was to be delivered to the funeral parlour in possession of Dr. Muñoz's remains. It was my understanding that the late physician's own wardrobe included no suitable burial attire, and as he had voiced his admiration--"

"But I say, Jeeves. The doc and I were hardly the same size." I am on the tall and willowy side, while the stiff barely scraped my coat-tails.

"In the circumstances, sir, a precise fit was not deemed essential."

"Jeeves, I say--"

"In the meantime, sir, if you desire a replacement, I recommend you patronise Howards Men's and Young Men's Clothes. A courteous salesman of my acquaintance there would be glad to show you their plain blue serge."

CHAPTER 3

The Rummy Affair of Young Charlie

LIFE IS a hideous thingummy. Take the case of Arthur "Pongo" Jermyn, for instance. Art was not like any other Egg, Bean, or Crumpet, for he was a poet and a dreamer, the sort of chappie who after a few quick ones would declare that the stars are God's daisy-chain, that every time a fairy hiccoughs a wee baby is born, and that we humans are not a separate species. This poetic lunacy fit right in with his *outré* personal appearance. It is easy to say just what the poor chimp--sorry, chump-- resembled. To swing across the Drones swimming-bath by the ropes and rings was with him the work of a moment, if you know what I mean. Even Tuppy Glossup's looping back the last ring did not cause Sir Arthur to drop into the fluid and ruin his specially tailored dress-clothes with the fifty-inch sleeves.

A sensitive bird, Art. Later that same night, after St. John speculated rather too freely on the unknown origins of his music-hall mother, he went out on the moor and set fire to his clothing. Spared the frying pan of the soup, his entire outfit, extra-long arms and all, was like the "mad truth" in the sonnet, "devoured by a flame." Unfortunately, so was my late pal, as the ass hadn't bothered to disrobe. I can assure you that those rumours about his first seeing a boxed *object* which had come from Africa are only so much rot. It was his looking like a supporting player out of an Edgar Rice Burroughs jungle thriller, not this *object* (which was merely the mummy of one of his white-ape ancestors), that led to his awful doom.

Yes, life can be a rummy thing--downright scaly, don't you know, as also shown by the case of Charles "Dexter" Ward. I had never heard of this Ward till the fateful day--one of those juicy late spring ones, with a seething, impenetrable sky of bluish coruscations--that my Aunt Agatha unexpectedly appeared on the doorstep.

"Mrs. Spenser Gregson to see you, sir," announced Jeeves.

"Oh gosh!" I said, shaken to the core. I had recently arisen from the abyss of sleep, and a surprise visit from Aunt Agatha was about as welcome as a midnight call from a reanimated corpse.

"Bertie!" exclaimed Aunt Agatha, following hot on the faithful servitor's heels. I noticed that she was looking somewhat pale and peaked, rather like Art Jermyn's great-great-great-grandmother.

"Oh hullo, old ancestor," I chirped. "Topping weather we've been having, what?"

"It is celibate bachelors like you, Bertie, who make a person realise why the human race will have to give way to the hardy coleopterous species. Instead of lolling about indoors this lovely morning you should be out chasing some charming girl in the Park."

"No, really, I say, please!" I said, blushing richly. Aunt Agatha owns two or three of these gent's magazines, and she keeps forgetting she isn't in an editorial meeting.

"Bertie, I didn't come here to lecture you on your lack of a sex life."

"Oh, no?"

"No. I had to see you immediately on a much graver matter. In today's post I received a most distressing letter from some dear American friends of mine, Mr. and Mrs. Theodore Howland Ward, of Providence, in New-England. They are extremely worried about their son Charles."

"Oh, yes?"

"Yes. A year ago, the senior Wards report, Charles determined after coming of age to take the European trip they had hitherto denied him. Before sailing for

Liverpool, he promised to write them fully and faithfully. Letters soon told of his safe arrival, and of his securing good quarters in Great Russell Street, London; where he proposed to stay till he had exhausted the resources of the British Museum in a certain direction."

"Sounds like a bookish cove."

"The alarming thing is, he has shunned all family friends."

"A shy bookish cove." While I didn't say so, with family friends like Aunt Agatha, the chap had probably avoided a lot of hell-and-high-water by cheesing the trans-Atlantic introductions.

"Of his daily life he wrote but little. Study and experiment consumed all his time, and he mentioned a laboratory which he had established in one of his rooms."

"I say, not a well-cooled laboratory!" I yipped, chilled to the marrow. The previous autumn in New York I'd run afoul of a blighter who enjoyed doing experiments in the home, and I was still reeling from the experience. Could this American chappie be a chip off the same iceberg?

"His last communication was a brief note telling of his departure for Paris."

"Flown the metrop., has he?" I said in some relief, for the conversation seemed to have been drifting towards Bertram's being called upon to roll out the welcome wagon--show the young blister the best and brightest night spots, lunch him at one's club, all that sort of thing. "Well, I'm sure that after a year of messing about museums in all directions, even a shy bookish cove would be ready to stampede to Paris like a ghoul to a graveyard."

"Bertie, it is imperative that you and Jeeves go to Paris right away. You must check up on the boy and do everything you can to keep him out of mischief."

"Yes, but I say..."

"Bertie!"

"But, dash it all..."

"I am counting on you, Bertie, not to let the Wards down. In my reply I shall tell them that you are already en route to Paris."

Further resistance was clearly useless, so once again in the face of superior force I hoisted the white flag and cried uncle--or in this case, aunt. After the triumphant withdrawal of the aged relative, I cast a mournful eye at Jeeves, who had been fooling with some silver in the background.

"I had better be packing, sir?"

"I suppose so."

I could see from the way he absent-mindedly slipped a spoon into his pocket that the man was not altogether satisfied with this turn in our affairs.

"Forgive me for saying so, sir," said Jeeves, "but it is my impression from Mrs. Gregson's remarks--"

"I know, Jeeves," I said, raising a restraining hand. "You're going to advise me not to throw caution to the wind and lope in on all-fours, but you can take it from me, one does not lightly or carelessly defy Aunt Agatha."

My experience is that when Aunt Agatha wants you to do a thing you do it, or else you find yourself wondering why the Old Ones made such a fuss when they had trouble with their shoggoths.

Paris, which we reached early the next day after a blasphemously choppy crossing and a noisome night in a train, fairly drips with gaiety and *joie de vivre* in the late spring, so I can't say that I was feeling too put out by the time we were settled at our hotel, a mere black-stone's throw away from Ward's own address in the Rue St. Jacques. Since I had no desire to venture over to his lodgings, where he might already be splashing the chemicals about the laboratory, I duly invited the lad to come round for tea *chez* Wooster. From his reply I could tell he was not keen on the prospect of accepting cucumber sandwiches from a stranger stooging for his people in Providence, but on the appointed afternoon he did pull in on schedule.

While an impartial observer would no doubt have considered the tall, slim bird that Jeeves ushered in a finer physical specimen than, say, Art Jermyn, there was about our visitor something quite (I hate to say this) bland. The handshake limp as a fish, the eye that resolutely refused to meet one's own, as well as the tendency to guzzle the tea and gobble the sandwiches like a schoolboy home on holiday, were but the more salient signs--or so this same impartial observer would be forced to conclude--that here was a fellow sorely out of practice in the social graces department.

"Well, well, well, Ward," I said, taking the avuncular approach. "Must be rather jolly, your first time to Paris, what?"

"Actually, it's not my first time to Paris."

"It's not?"

"Nope. From London I made one or two flying trips for material in the Bibliothèque Nationale."

"Oh, ah, yes, of course. Our English material's never good enough for you Americans, so you pop over to Paris for French material in the Biblio-what's-it... Er, just what sort of material?"

"Nothing much really, just some stuff to do with my research."

"Research?"

"Yup, research."

"May I ask what kind of research?"

"Um, let me see now. I guess you could call it antiquarian research."

"You mean you're one of these collector blokes like my Uncle Tom who covets things like eighteenth-century silver cow-creamers?"

"Well, um, not exactly. I am pretty interested in old books and stuff like that, though. Right now I'm doing a special search among rare manuscripts in the library of a private collector."

"A private collector? Maybe he knows my Uncle Tom. Mind my asking his name?"

"Well, I don't want to sound rude or anything, but I think it's better if I, um, just keep the guy's name to myself. Okay?"

I have always found that given half a chance most Americans on first acquaintance will spill their life stories and then some. Such, however, was not the case with Charlie Ward. Only when I touched on the hometown topic of Providence, Rhode Island, did he drop the mask and bare the soul a bit--though it did strike me as rum that a non-university man should wax rhapsodic over a place called College Hill.

"See here, Ward," I said, as our guest swabbed the last drops of tea out of his saucer with the last crust of sandwich bread. "You can take this shy bookish pose only so far. Instead of palling around with unnamed private collectors, you should be out stalking pretty girls in the Bois de Boulogne. At least that's what you can bet my Aunt Agatha would recommend."

"Gosh, Mr. Wooster, it's sure nice of you to give me all this free advice. I'll consider it real carefully. Okay? In the meantime, thanks *mucho* for the grub. *Adios*."

After our visitor tottered off, I turned to Jeeves for his assessment.

"Well, Jeeves, what do you make of the lad?"

"In my opinion, sir, the gentleman's studious eyes and slight stoop, together with his somewhat careless dress, give a dominant impression of harmless awkwardness rather than attractiveness."

"Short on attractiveness and long on awkwardness, yes, that's our boy in a nutshell, Jeeves. But harmless? Ha!" I laughed. One of those short ironic ones. "If you ask me, unless he cleans up his act, young Charlie could do more harm than a resurrected wizard left alone in a sandbox of essential saltes."

Over the fortnight that followed, I set about with the zeal of a missionary among the heathen to reveal to the reclusive New Englander the error of his unwholesome ways. Dining at fine restaurants was a wash-out, as the chap had an unholy suspicion of any and all unfamiliar food. Unlike the cucumber sandwiches which proved so boffo, the *ris de Dhole à la Financière* and the *velouté aux fleurs de Tcho-Tcho* went untasted on the platter. Wines were wasted as well, as he confessed to being a confirmed teetotaler. Similarly, outings to the Auteuil race course and to the

Roville-sur-mer casinos only served to show that my Puritanical companion possessed not a drop of sporting blood. In short, he displayed none of the youthful ebullience which, for example, inflamed my cousins, Claude and Eustace, that time they descended on the metrop. from Oxford to pinch cats and policemen's helmets.

Only once, when he persuaded Jeeves and myself to play a parlour game called "Shoes and Socks," did my charge betray a spark of *esprit*. But even this was a bust, as the proceedings came to a screeching halt when he discovered I had travelled to the C. *sans* Bible. Assurances that I had won the prize for Scripture Knowledge at my private school did not appease. In the end Jeeves and I suffered no little embarrassment retrieving our footwear from the *gamin* on whom they had fallen when Ward dropped them out the hotel window in a sack.

"Jeeves, we're up against it this time," I declared in the aftermath of the shoes and socks episode. "If only Aunt Agatha weren't so bally set on saving the silly sap's soul, I'd chuck the case as fast as Charlie tossed the spats and garters *dans la rue*." On Aunt Agatha's orders, which arrived almost daily, I had been despatching regular progress reports. I knew that today's news from the French front would get a cool reception at G.H.Q. London.

"Speaking of Mrs. Gregson, sir, she enclosed in her morning *communiqué* a missive from the Ward family physician, a Dr. Marinus Bicknell Willett. I have taken the liberty of perusing the contents. You may find, sir, that it sheds some light on the psychology of the individual."

"Why don't you just give me the gist, Jeeves."

"Very good, sir," the man replied, his usual solemn tone shading into the sepulchral. "Dr. Willett discloses that the youth underwent a three-year period of intensive occult study and graveyard searching before leaving for England."

"Hm, if I'm not mistaken, Jeeves, didn't that New York chum of mine also have a thing about graveyards?"

"Yes, sir. As you may recall, sir, Mr. Carter reportedly had a most unpleasant encounter in an unknown and archaic--"

"Yes, yes, never mind the sordid details. Pray continue, Jeeves. What other tit-bits does this Doc Willett have to offer about the patient?"

"Once, sir" intoned Jeeves, "he went south to talk with a strange old mulatto who dwelt in a swamp."

"I say, not the same chap with whom Randy used to share a study, do you suppose?"

"Dr. Willett does not make the association, sir."

"Quite suggestive, though, Jeeves, what?"

"Indeed, sir."

"Anything else, Jeeves?"

"Yes, sir. In addition, the young gentleman sought a small village in the Adirondacks whence reports of certain odd ceremonial practices had come."

"These are deep waters, Jeeves," I said, tenting the fingertips. "Or rather, high hills. Have you any clue to their meaning?"

"Arthur Machen, sir, has written of odd ceremonial practices among the natives of the Welsh hill country. I can well imagine villagers in the remote mountain areas of the United States of America also engaging in such practices."

"Well, Jeeves," I said, after brooding a bit on the ceremonial concept, "at this stage of the investigation only one thing is certain."

"And what may that be, sir?"

"That young Ward would be warmly received at any private hospital for the insane."

"The latest evidence, sir, would seem to support the notion that Mr. Ward is an exceedingly singular person."

"If it weren't for that cats-and-rats, er, cats-and-fish-in-the-bedroom business, I would immediately wire Sir Roderick Glossup: 'Loony American loose in Paris. Please reserve next available padded cell.'"

"I daresay, sir, we may yet require professional assistance."

*

The next development in the rummy affair of young Charlie seemed to augur the light before the dawn. The blighter disappeared, leaving behind no forwarding address. I was all set to throw in the towel and call it a day, when Aunt Agatha herself blew in for a surprise inspection. The old flesh and blood promised that she would have up "ye Legions from Underneath" and sic them on B. Wooster, unless he hopped to and resumed the chase: "All civilisation, all natural law, perhaps even the fate of the solar system and the universe depend on your following through, you miserable worm." Never one to mince words, Aunt Agatha, even if she did rather overstate the case.

So there was nothing for it but to give Jeeves his head and see if he could run our elusive scholar to ground. And by Jove, within the week he had sniffed out the lad's new lair, at a rooming-house in the Rue d'Auseil.

"Yoicks, Jeeves!" I ejaculated when the man announced that the quarry was at bay. "I mean to say, excellent!"

"I endeavour to give satisfaction, sir."

"So, Jeeves, our boy's holed up in the Rue d'Auseil. Is that by chance anywhere near the Auteuil race course?"

"No, sir. If you must know, sir, I experienced no small difficulty discovering Mr. Ward's present whereabouts."

"Oh, yes?"

"The Rue d'Auseil is not down in any map, sir."

"Oh, no?"

"No, sir. As Melville says, sir, true places never are."

"Like that lost city in Africa Art Jermyn was always gassing about, I suppose. But I say, Jeeves, let's stick to the *res*. What other data did you dig up?"

"Mr. Ward has ceased to affiliate with the private collector whose name he refused to divulge, sir. On the other hand, sir, it appears that his removal to the Rue d'Auseil was prompted by the desire to associate with yet another unusual individual."

"Were you able to scare up a name for this chap?"

"Yes, sir. The gentleman in question signs his name as Erich Zann. He is an old German viol-player, sir, a strange dumb man who plays evenings in a cheap theatre orchestra."

"Really, Jeeves, is this Zann's playing so vile that he has to settle for music halls featuring the likes of Art Jermyn's mother?"

Nothing against Mrs. Jermyn personally, of course, despite all those frightful rumours St. John used to spread about the Drones, but you know the kind of chorus girl I mean.

"You misapprehend me, sir. A viol is a bowed stringed instrument with deep body, flat back, sloping shoulders, six strings, fretted fingerboard, low-arched bridge--"

"Please, Jeeves," I said, lifting a warning hand. "Your musical knowledge may be *nonpareil*, but we're once again wandering far afield. What in the dickens do you suppose Ward sees in this clammed-up codger?"

"I could not say, sir, as I have not spoken with the young gentleman. My informant, however, is not sanguine about Herr Zann's influence."

"Your informant?"

"Yes, sir. A third tenant of the house in the Rue d'Auseil, an elderly American and vigilant observer of the domestic scene, has been kind enough to supply the essential background information."

"One of these Nosy Parkers, eh?"

"You might say so, sir, although I believe his motives to be above reproach. Once I explained our situation *vis à vis* Mr. Ward, he proposed that we combine forces."

"Very good, Jeeves. But, I say, do you think we can trust this American buster? Can he deliver the goods?"

"He impressed me as a person on whom we can confidently rely in matters of the utmost delicacy, sir. Indeed, sir, I have taken the liberty of arranging a meeting to discuss how best to coordinate our efforts."

"Hasn't been reticent about revealing his name, has he?"

"Pardon me, sir, I should have mentioned it earlier." Jeeves gave one of those discreet coughs of his, like a sheep clearing its throat in the spray from an Alpine waterfall. "The gentleman introduces himself as Mr. Altamont, of Chicago."

The following forenoon Jeeves ushered into the presence a tall, gaunt chappie of seventy, sporting a tuft of chin-fuzz which gave him a general resemblance to the mug shots of Uncle Sam. Not my Uncle Sam, mind you, whose phiz I used to render in crayon at the risk of a trashing as a tot, but the American imitation of our own John Bull.

"Howdy, mister," said the man, slapping the shoulder with a rough familiarity from which I shied like a startled faun. One can be mistaken in these things, of course, but this Altamont didn't strike me off-hand as the sort of johnny on whose utmost delicacy one could confidently rely.

"Oh, ah. The pleasure is all mine, old bean," I said, betraying no horror as the gargoyle poured his longish limbs into an armchair with not so much as a by-your-leave and relit a half-smoked, sodden cigar.

"It's Mr. Wooster, ain't it?" exclaimed the Irish-American. "Mr. Jeeves said you were pretty regular for a swell, the kind of fella you can count on to help bring home the bacon."

"As Jeeves will attest," I retorted, "I am extremely fond of the eggs and b. But you should understand, my dear chap, that it is my man who does all the grocery shopping for the household."

"Hey, no offense, mister. I just meant to say you're a dude who sticks by his guns, a guy who when the chips are down will walk the last mile for a pal."

"Well, we Woosters do have our code, don't you know," I murmured, all very dignified and feudal.

"I'm not one to brag much, mister, but I've cracked a few codes in my day, too--a hundred and sixty all told. There was this one cipher that this gang in Chicago--"

"Chicago!" I cried. "Your native burg, is it not?"

"You bet, mister."

"The city that many of the *cognescenti* consider the crime capital of the Western Hemisphere," I continued. "Home of speakeasies, bootleg liquor, Tommy guns, *Weird Tales* magazine, what?"

"Gosh, I wont deny--"

"Al Capone wouldn't by chance be a pal of yours, would he?"

"Ha, ha," the man laughed, the stogie bobbing above the chin-fungus. "You implyin' I hang out with crooks? Believe me, friend, every now and then I act independent of the coppers, but I always land feet first on the right side of the law."

"I can assure you I sail a pretty straight course myself," I responded, "except on Boat-Race Night. I usually go for a swim in the Trafalgar Square fountain, which offence rates a five-pound fine from the Bosher Street beak."

"Glad to hear you ain't above cutting a caper on occasion, mister."

Having hit on a common interest in the criminal impulse, I have to admit I found myself warming to the bloke, with his bluff, easy manner. Not that I was about to bet my little all on his utmost delicacy with any confidence, but I decided he at least deserved a hearing.

"See here, Alamont," I said at last. "Jeeves tells me you've got the dope on young Ward in his new digs. Just what's the posish. and what do you propose we do?"

"Well, mister, here's the lowdown," the man replied, laying the remains of his cigar to rest in his breastpocket. "It so happens Charlie and I'd both like to sink our hooks into a certain manuscript belonging to this Zann fella."

"Right, the deaf, dumb, blind bird Jeeves was giving me the scoop on."

"It'd be a gol-darned shame if Zann's manuscript was to fall into the wrong hands--"

"I say, you're not another one of these collector types, are you?"

"No, sirree--though I used to do quite a business in my heyday tracking down stolen documents. Putting the finger on missing top-secret government papers was a specialty of mine."

"Are you going to suggest we pinch the thing? If so, I have to say I've got some experience in this line of larceny." I proceeded to relate how I once tried to intercept the manuscript of my Uncle Willoughby's reminiscences, which were full of stories about people who are the essence of propriety today being chucked out of music halls and such like back in the 'eighties. The anecdote about Art Jermyn's father, the itinerant American circus, and the huge bull gorilla of lighter than average colour was one of the fruitiest.

"Should be a piece of cake to slip into the gimp's room and filch the foolscap," I added. "Like taking fish from a Deep One, I should think."

"It ain't that simple, mister," said Altamont. "The catch is, the manuscript ain't down on paper yet--the swag's upstairs, stashed inside Herr Zann's noggin."

"I say, that does make for somewhat more of a challenge, doesn't it?"

"This is how I figure it. To get the guy to play ball, you have to play him the way an Indian snake charmer does a deadly swamp adder."

"Oh, ah, of course," I answered, though I hadn't the foggiest what he was driving at.

"'Music hath charm to soothe the savage beast' I recollect is the old saw," said Altamont in explanation.

"Excuse me, sir," said Jeeves, who shimmered in at that moment, "but I believe that the line from Congreve is 'Music has charms to soothe a savage breast.'"

"Thank you, Jeeves," I said, "but as you can see--"

"Say, your man here's one sharp cookie, mister," Altamont interjected. "I knew it when we met--he had to be the brains behind your operation."

Jeeves may be the Napoleon of valets, but we Woosters have our pride, don't you know, so I let the remark pass.

"Anyhow," continued the American, "I've tried all by my lonesome on my fiddle to coax Zann to ante up, but no dice. Charlie, on the other hand, hasn't had any better luck tooting on that zobo of his."

"I say, but where do I come in?" I was still as much in the dark as that chap Washington after the lights went out, but I was beginning to get a glimmer that a plum role awaited Bertram in this affair.

"Mr. Jeeves says you can belt out a tune with the best of 'em."

"I took the liberty of informing Mr. Altamont that you have a pleasant, light baritone, sir."

"What'll turn the trick, I reckon, is if we spring a little jam session on Zann some night, all impromptu like. I'll wager my wad that if we serenade the old duffer with a medley of mus c-hall melodies, he'll be ready by dawn to deliver the goods. So how about it, miste-? Can I count you in?"

Well, I mean to say, this was a bit thick. After performing "Sonny Boy" at Beefy Bingham's clean, bright entertainment in the East End, I had sworn off singing outside the privacy of my own bath. Now I was being called upon to lead a chorus in a scheme as hare-brained as any I had heard in a goodish while. Then I thought of Aunt Agatha and what she would say and do if she found out I had funked this latest gag to fish young Ward out of the soup, and at that instant I resolved to take the plunge and seize the rising tide across the Rubicon, so to speak.

"All right, then," I declared. "Why not?"

An evening or two later, by the light of a gibbous moon, Jeeves and I were crossing not the Rubicon but a dark, ripe-smelling river spanned by a low-arched bridge as ponderous as Jeeves's definition of the word *viol*. *Vile*, too, was the word that sprang to the lips when we entered the neighbourhood that lay beyond. An antiquarian's paradise I know some would call it, but plague spot would be more the *mot juste*. In my view the whole tangle of narrow cobbled streets and crazily leaning houses was in dire need of the wrecker's ball. Moreover, the Rue d'Auseil itself was aswarm with doddering greybeards who looked as if they'd been pensioned off from Napoleon's Grande Armée. No wonder the place wasn't down in any map.

We stopped at the third tottering house from the top of the street, an edifice that in tallishness rivalled the Eiffel Tower. At the door we were greeted by the chap who kept the joint, an ancient bird with bum legs named Blandot. As he directed us *en haut*, he wished us *bonne chance*. I had assumed that this was to be a strictly private concert, but the landlord made it clear that Monsieur Altamont's musical soirée was the talk of the house and we could expect an avid audience.

Like an obedient bloodhound, Jeeves took the lead upstairs, pausing on the third floor to point towards Ward's apartment. As we trotted higher, the long sob of a violin pierced our hearts and ears, and when we gained the fifth floor we found waiting on the landing our American confederate, stringèd instrument clasped to the bosom.

"Howdy, folks!" the geezer wheezed, slapping us each on the back as best he could with bow in one hand and violin in the other. "Come on in!"

Our new friend steered us inside his room, where our noses were instantly assaulted by the reek of stale cigar smoke, not to mention other evil stenches which I have never smelled elsewhere (with the possible exception of Doc Muñoz's Fourteenth Street bedsitter) but which seemed to emanate from the test tubes and retorts that filled every nook and cranny of the otherwise Spartanly furnished premises.

"I say, you're not one of these chaps who, who like to..." I stammered, gripped by a nameless fear.

"Well, mister, I guess you could say experimentin's kind of a hobby of mine, just as it is Charlie's, by the way. He and I have even swapped a few recipes, er, formulas..."

Most disturbing, as Jeeves would say, was the fact that there was no source of running water within eyeballing distance. Running water, as any Etonian will tell you, is as much of the essence to the chemistry lab as fresh blood is to the vampire.

Jeeves, no doubt sensing the young master's distress, had some soothing words at the ready. "Observe, sir," said the man in a low, buzzing whisper, "that Mr. Altamont at least does not maintain a well-chilled laboratory."

Rather the opposite, one might add. In truth, Altamont's quarters were about as warmly oppressive as a sealed tomb on a summer's day. When I suggested, however, that an open window might be just the ticket, our host said no, an open window wasn't a smart idea on the Rue d'Auseil. So I resigned self to the fact that our rehearsal--we had a few hours to practice before Zann's return--would be a sticky business in more ways than one.

While I was fiddling with the sheet music which I'd purchased for the occasion--and a dashed lot of bother it was too, hunting up English lyrics at short notice in a foreign capital--Altamont asked: "You play an instrument, mister?"

"No, never have, my dear fellow, though now that you mention it," I said, casting Jeeves a meaningful glance, "I've always wanted to have a go at learning the banjolele." At this revelation Jeeves's left eyebrow may have flickered a quarter of an inch.

"Well, well, that's fine," replied Altamont. "Now what would you like to let your lungs loose on first? 'Old Man River' or 'The Yeoman's Wedding Song'?"

Barely had I cleared the throat and Altamont given a final twist to the G-string, when suddenly there came a tapping, a tentative, gentle sort of rapping, as the poet says, at the chamber door. At a nod from our host, Jeeves flew as swiftly and silently as a raven to see who was there.

"Hey, you guys weren't going to start without me, were you?" whined a peevish--if that's the word I want--Ward on the threshold. "I am a star zobo soloist, you know." In one hand he brandished a zobo, not an especially impressive weapon, mind you, but by the authoritative way he flourished the thing I could tell that he didn't care to be left out of the proceedings.

"Now, now, Charlie, simmer down," said Altamont. "Say, why don't you come on in?"

"Thanks. Um, don't mind if I do," said Ward, sounding as if he were merely accepting his due as a paid-up member in good standing of our little club.

Well, the long and short of it was, after a hasty huddle between Jeeves and Altamont, we opened up our ranks and expanded from a duo to a trio. As it turned out, the mellow fruitiness of Charlie's zobo playing enriched the ensemble beyond measure, and I for one was not sorry to have him aboard. At one point, while Altamont was performing a solo, Jeeves whispered out of Ward's earshot that the elderly American had half-expected this contingency, indeed was prepared to grab "the bacon" and execute an "end run" under the younger American's very nose if he had to. His solo, incidentally, had that quality which I have noticed in all violin solos, of seeming to last much longer than it actually did.

By eleven o'clock, while we were far from fit to make our debut at the Albert Hall, we had our act well enough together to transfer it to Zann's garret, which was strategically located one floor directly above.

"For your information," said Altamont, as we mounted the rickety attic stairs, "a college kid who lived here a few years back almost got the old boy to cough up, but the bonehead blew it..."

"It is my understanding that the young gentleman was an impoverished student of metaphysics at the university, sir," said Jeeves.

A pass-key provided courtesy of Blandot allowed us to slip without fuss into Zann's room. Its size was very great, and seemed the greater because of its extraordinary barrenness and neglect. I mean to say, the abundance of dust and cobwebs would have embarrassed even Mrs. Herrero, Doc Muñoz's last landlady and housekeeper *manqué*. The fans soon began to trickle in, first the lame landlord then a pair of chaps from the third floor, an aged money-lender and a respectable upholsterer. The performers clustered round an iron music-rack, while the audience settled in three old-fashioned chairs and on the narrow iron bedstead. Despite a complaint or two about the lack of a programme, the mood of the crowd was on the whole relaxed and cheery. Finally, near midnight, the estimated kick-off time, Altamont gave Jeeves the signal to douse the lights, saying, "Now we must be silent and wait, gents."

After what seemed like fifteen minutes but from comparing notes afterwards was but forty-five seconds, we heard a clumping on the stairs, the grating of a key in the lock, and the creak of the swinging door. When the light flashed on it was all we could do to restrain ourselves from shouting surprise at the old maestro, who stood gaping in astonishment like a crook caught red-handed (or is it red-headed?) breaking into a bank vault *from beneath.*

He was a small, lean, bent person, with the shabby clothes of a vaudeville comedian and a nearly bald head like the dome of St. Paul's or, if my Providence pal were telling this tale, like the dome of the Christian Science Church on College Hill. The silent way he started to get worked up, making funny faces and shaking the sinister black viol case he was carrying, rather reminded me of Harpo Marx, minus the fright wig. One couldn't help wondering whether he'd ever considered billing himself as "Violo" Zann.

"Come on, Herr Zann," said Altamont, dragging the German by the elbow to a free spot on the bedstead, "be a sport. Tonight we're entertaining you."

Over the old man's mute protests, Altamont rejoined Ward and me at the music-rack and raised his bow. On the downbeat we launched into "The Wedding of the Painted Doll," which drew appreciative applause at the finish from all hands except Zann's. Thus encouraged, we proceeded with growing confidence to perform "Singin' in the Rain," "Three Little Words," "Goodnight, Sweetheart," "My Love Parade," "Spring Is Here," "Whose Baby Are You?" and part of "I Want an Automobile with a Horn That Goes Toot-Toot," in the order named.

It was as we were approaching the end of this last number that Zann suddenly rose, seized his viol, and commenced to rend the night with the wildest playing I had ever heard outside the amateur musical evenings at the Drones. It would be useless to describe the playing of Erich Zann further, so I won't. In any case, the bloke shortly dropped the viol and stumbled over to the room's lone table, where he picked up a pencil and began to write like a compulsive epistolarian. (For a poor musician,

he fortuitously kept reams of writing paper in the home.) We resumed our playing, which accompaniment seemed to drive the eccentric genius to pile up the feverishly written sheets at an ever faster clip. As the wee hours wore on, Ward and Altamont watched his progress with an increasingly lean and hungry eye.

I had just hit the opening quaver of "Sonny Boy" when young Charlie missed his cue. Out of the gate like a shot, he bounded to the table and was shovelling the manuscript pages into a bag before you could say John Clay. Zann, who was beginning to look a trifle glassy-eyed, seemed scarcely to notice the intrusion. Altamont, himself no spring chicken, was slow to blow the whistle. "Whoa, Bill!" he cried after a tick or two. "Up and at him, lads!"

The audience rose as one, though not with any appreciable alacrity. Both the money-lender and the upholsterer were past their prime, while a tortoise could have given bum-legged Blandot a run for his money. Nonetheless, this team--all presumably Altamont's accomplices--succeeded in tackling Ward and bringing him down short of his goal, the door, which Jeeves, who had moved like a phantom, was now tending. The contestants soon formed a scrum, with Charlie taking on all comers, a sort of Samson among the Philistines, if you will. Altamont, like archaic Nodens, bellowed his guidance from the sidelines.

And where, you may ask, was Bertram in the crisis? I had posted self by the room's one window, waiting in reserve as the good old ancestor did during the early phase of the Battle of Crécy. As the atmosphere grew foul with the dust and cobwebs kicked up in the struggle for the ms, I decided it would be a sound scheme to open the window, despite Altamont's previous admonition against same. So I drew back the curtains, unlatched the shutter, and raised the sash of that highest of all gable windows.

Before I could admire the view, however, Fate socked me with the stuffed eelskin. That is to say, something soft and loose struck the old occiput. I turned to see that Ward had scattered most of the opposition about the floor like nine pins. Zann in particular was looking poorly, eyes springing out of the sockets and ricocheting off the ceiling. Then I noticed the object of everyone's quest--which must have flown free in the fray--lying at the feet.

My course of action was clear. Charlie had just broken out of a clinch with Altamont and was now advancing menacingly in my direction. It was the work of a moment to sweep up the prize and drop it out the window, just as Ward did that time with the bag full of Jeeves's and my footwear. Except in this case, there was something rum about the outside view. It was very dark, but instead of the lights of the city outspread below, I saw-- But how shall I describe it? I don't know if you've ever stared long and hard into one of those swirling spiral thingummies which hypnotists like to poke in people's faces, but such was the image registering on the Wooster retina. Entrancing, you might say. Dashed entrancing. So entrancing I--

"Well, Jeeves," I was saying in the aftermath of our little adventure, back at the clean and comfortable hotel suite, "all's well that end's well, I suppose."

"Yes, sir. I would agree that Mr. Ward's precipitous departure for Prague absolves you of any further responsibility for his welfare."

"I can't help feeling a pang for old Altamont, though. A pity that Zann's confessions, as well as the venerable musician himself, have passed beyond the gulf beyond the gulf beyond..."

"In my opinion, sir, Mr. Altamont will in time not be wholly sorry for the loss in undreamable abysses of Herr Zann's closely written manuscript."

"I say, Jeeves, what do you imagine Zann poured out on the page and why were Ward and Altamont so keen on seizing the contents? Any clue?"

"None, sir. Like the book cited by Poe's German authority, sir, '*es lasst sich nicht lesen*--it does not permit itself to be read.'"

The Adventure of the Three Anglo-American Authors:

Some Reflections on Conan Doyle, P. G. Wodehouse, and H. P. Lovecraft

AFTER dismissing mysteries in general in his *New Yorker* essay, "'Mr. Holmes, They Were the Footprints of a Gigantic Hound!'" (1945), Edmund Wilson says of the fictional detective: "My contention is that Sherlock Holmes *is* literature on a humble but not ignoble level, whereas the mystery writers most in vogue now are not. The old stories are literature, not because of the conjuring tricks and the puzzles, which they have in common with many other detective stories, but by virtue of imagination and style. These are fairy-tales, as Conan Doyle intimated in his preface to his last collection, and they are among the most amusing of fairy-tales and not among the least distinguished." So too, by virtue of imagination and style, do the comedies of P. G. Wodehouse rank as literature; and so as well do the dark fantasies or "fairy-tales" of H. P. Lovecraft, though Wilson would demur (see his fatheaded *New Yorker* essay published later in 1945, "Tales of the Marvellous and the Ridiculous").

Arthur Conan Doyle (1859-1930), Pelham Grenville Wodehouse (1881-1975), and Howard Phillips Lovecraft (1890-1937), I contend, stand at the head of their respective genres--mystery, humor, and horror. Note first that the supreme fictional achievements of each are roughly comparable in size: Doyle's Sherlock Holmes canon consists of 56 stories and four novels; Wodehouse's Jeeves saga embraces 34 stories and 11 novels; and Lovecraft's core corpus, including his Mythos cycle, amounts to two dozen or so stories and three novels. Such a superficial parallel proves nothing, of course, yet a survey of the connections between and among this in some ways unlikely triumvirate and their work is, I believe, not without its instructive points.

To address one obvious disparity from the start, the link between Doyle and Wodehouse, who for one thing knew each other personally, is far stronger and clearer, I admit, than any tie either might have to Lovecraft. Of the trio the American could be said to be the odd-man out, chiefly due to the relatively narrow appeal of the supernatural tale. In their lifetimes both Sir Arthur and Sir Pelham, as prolific and popular authors, enjoyed enormous commercial success. They could afford, for example, to belong to clubs. (And so too could the characters in their stories. Sherlock Holmes's brother, Mycroft, is a member of the Diogenes, while Bertie Wooster is a member of the Drones.) The Gentleman of Providence, Rhode Island, could never come close to earning a living from his original fiction. Revision work often amounting to ghostwriting provided a more reliable source of income. Apart from a shoddy fan-press edition of "The Shadow Over Innsmouth," no book of his was published in his lifetime. The only men's club he belonged to was the Kalem Club, an informal literary circle of which he was the leading light during his two years of New York exile. (In his fiction there is but a single reference to a club--the Miskatonic, where the narrator of "The Thing on the Doorstep" does not like what the protagonist's banker lets fall in an overexpansive mood regarding the protagonist's finances.) If Lovecraft has achieved a measure of posthumous fame, it remains modest by comparison to theirs.

Lovecraft also stands apart because he rarely catered to the masses. Some have asserted that as a self-consciously serious artist, he sought mainly to express his peculiar, what S. T. Joshi would call his "cosmic," world view. Unlike the other two, he cared more about satisfying an aesthetic ideal than pleasing his readers. Nonetheless, as Will Murray properly reminds us, his stories remain, whatever their claim to philosophical profundity, popular entertainments, worthy to be considered, I like to think, in the company of the masterpieces of his more illustrious literary kin.

A COMMON APPEAL

An enthusiasm for at least two of these authors is commonplace, in fact, and a taste for all three not without precedent. The man who preserved Lovecraft in hardcover, August Derleth, wrote the Solar Pons pastiches (as well as a dozen or so "posthumous collaborations" with HPL). Fantasist Lin Carter, another chronic imitator, left behind an uncompleted manuscript in the Wodehouse vein. The late Isaac Asimov was not only a great Sherlockian but also a keen Wodehousian. Philip Shreffler, author of the *Lovecraft Companion*, has edited the Baker Street Irregulars' periodical, the *Baker Street Journal*--in which horror writer Manley Wade Wellman once argued that Jeeves is the offspring of Sherlock Holmes and his landlady Mrs. Hudson.

Sherlockian Vincent Starrett, who promoted the weird work of Arthur Machen in the 1920s, admired Lovecraft's stories in *Weird Tales*. The year Ben Abramson issued the first number of the *Baker Street Journal*, 1945, he published as a book HPL's long essay, *Supernatural Horror in Literature*. Closer to our own time best-selling phenomenon Stephen King, who has acknowledged his debt to Lovecraft, has penned a Holmes pastiche, "The Doctor's Case," as has actor-author Stephen Fry--"The Adventure of the Laughing Jarvey"--who has portrayed Jeeves in the current British TV series "Jeeves and Wooster." Sherlock Holmes confronts Cthulhu and other Lovecraftian creatures in two small-press pastiches by Ralph Vaughn. In 1992 followers of both the great detective and Bertie and Jeeves formed an "ambidextrous scion society," the Clients of Adrian Mulliner. As such examples suggest, something is definitely afoot here.

What accounts for this common appeal? Broadly speaking, all three men wrote stories that, however formulaic, play in rich and ingenious ways with a few stock elements of setting, character, and plot. At their best they each provided the pleasure of the familiar, with just the right amount of variation. Each imagined a distinctive time and place--Sherlock Holmes's late Victorian London, Bertie Wooster's Edwardian (with touches of Jazz Age) England, Lovecraft's decadent 1920s and '30s New England--free of ordinary cares and responsibilities. The male heroes of these boyish realms need never trouble themselves with realistic grown-up concerns of love and marriage, money and career. Even after he weds, Watson is ever ready to leave home and accompany Holmes on his latest case. Jeeves sees to it that Bertie never falls into the matrimonial trap. Lovecraft's one character to run afoul of a woman, Edward Derby of "The Thing on the Doorstep," lives (and dies and lives again) to regret the liaison. Nobody has a sex life.

It comes as no surprise that Wodehouse, a mystery enthusiast, viewed the dearth of romantic interest in the Holmes stories as a virtue while lamenting its prominence in later detective fiction. In his autobiographical *Over Seventy*, he confessed: "What we liked so much about Sherlock Holmes was his correct attitude in this matter of girls. True, he would sometimes permit them to call at Baker Street and tell him about the odd behaviour of their uncles or stepfathers ... in a pinch he might even allow them to marry Watson ... but once the story was under way they had to retire to the background and stay there. That was the spirit." It comes equally as no surprise that realistic relationships between the sexes should be absent from his own fiction. According to Frances Donaldson, his official biographer, his lack of attractive male characters (apart from some lame leading-men types in earlier works) accounts for why "out of every ten Wodehouse addicts only one will be a woman." She adds, "I am not myself naturally an aficionado."

One typically discovers Sherlock Holmes as a pre-adolescent, about age twelve or thirteen. More than a hundred years after his debut, the detective can still inspire devotion in the young bordering on worship. Stephen Fry, for example, says in his book *Paperweight* (1992) that as a schoolboy he was "the youngest member of the Sherlock Holmes Society of London. For a few thrilling, mad, exultant years I lived and breathed Sherlock Holmes to the exclusion of all other lives and oxygens." Boys often become enamored of Lovecraft at a similar impressionable age. In America at least, if one does encounter Wodehouse--and many literate persons today never do--it is not until well into adolescence or after. The truth is, Bertie and Jeeves take a more sophisticated sensibility to appreciate. To the youthful eye, their comic adventures appear mild by comparison to the exploits of Holmes and Watson or the cosmic chaos of Cthulhu. Unlike Doyle and Lovecraft, Wodehouse can be fully enjoyed only by adult readers.

Of course, the fictional creations of Doyle and Lovecraft excite their respective juvenile audiences in fundamentally different ways. Edmund Wilson speaks of the atmosphere of "cozy peril," a phrase he borrows from Christopher Morley, in regard to Holmes and Watson, who "will, of course, get safely back to Baker Street, after their vigils and raids and arrests, to discuss the case comfortably in their rooms and have their landlady bring them breakfast the next morning. Law and Order have not tottered a moment; the British police are well in control.... All the loose ends of every episode are tidily picked up and tucked in, and even Holmes, though once addicted to cocaine, has been reformed by the excellent Watson." The good doctor, incidentally, never explains why his friend eventually says no to drugs. The detective's cocaine habit, at any rate, stands out as the most unpleasant feature of the adventures, provoking the editors of *The Boys' Sherlock Holmes* to delete the opening account of Holmes shooting up from *The Sign of the Four* (which as a boy I always thought started a bit abruptly until I later read the full, unexpurgated text).

One could almost say that an atmosphere of "cozy peril" characterizes Lovecraft's stories, but here it is his readers who are at a safe remove, not his protagonists who, even if they escape the clutches of the cosmic monsters they uncover, are apt either to go insane or forever lose their peace of mind. (Grisly violence is rare in Lovecraft, and when it does occur, as in "The Thing on the Doorstep," it tends to be suggestive rather than explicit.) In a tale like "The Call of Cthulhu" natural law and order are shown to be shams. The police can do nothing. The horror is thwarted only temporarily. Of course, Lovecraft's dire vision of the "true" state of the world (and the universe) is as much romantic nonsense as Doyle's and Wodehouse's happier, more innocent views. To the adolescent sensibility that delights in anarchy, however, it can be more fun to see law and order ultimately upset instead of upheld.

A CASE OF INFLUENCE: SHERLOCK HOLMES

Writing to his friend Bill Townend in 1925, Wodehouse says of his hero Conan Doyle, "I still revere his work as much as ever. I used to think it swell, and I still think it swell. ... And apart from the work, I admire Doyle so much as a man. I should call him definitely a great man, and I don't imagine I'm the only one who thinks so. I love that solid, precise way he has of talking, like Sherlock Holmes." According to Barry Phelps, author of *P. G. Wodehouse: Man and Myth* (1992), the two men became friends in 1903 playing cricket. This association led to the young journalist interviewing the older, established writer for an article called "Grit. A Talk with Sir Arthur Conan Doyle." When Doyle resurrected Holmes in the autumn of that year, Wodehouse composed a poem in celebration, "Back to His Native Strand." Still other pieces from this period reflect his appreciation of Sir Arthur.

More than a half century later, a Mulliner story, "From a Detective's Notebook," suggests that Holmes invented his nemesis, Professor Moriarty, for his own convenience. In *Right Ho, Jeeves*, Jeeves invokes "Sir Arthur Conan Doyle's fictional detective, Sherlock Holmes." In fact, hundreds of such allusions crop up throughout Wodehouse's fiction, as both Sherlockians and Wodehousians have commented, including J. Randolph Cox in his *Baker Street Journal* essay, "'Elementary, My Dear Wooster!'" (1967). Cox acknowledges his debt to Richard Usborne, who is especially eloquent on the topic in his *Penguin Wodehouse Companion* (1988): "I seem to keep finding, or I keep seeming to find, trace elements of Conan Doyle in the Wodehouse formulations. I sense a distinct similarity, in patterns and rhythms, between the adventures of Jeeves as recorded by Bertie Wooster and the adventures of Sherlock Holmes as recorded by Doctor Watson: Holmes and Jeeves the great brains, Watson and Bertie the awed companion-narrators, bungling things if they try to solve the problems themselves; the problems, waiting to be tackled almost always in country houses, almost always presented and discussed at breakfast in London; the departure from London, Holmes and Watson by train, Jeeves and Bertie by two-seater; the gathering of the characters at the country house; the gathering of momentum, Holmes seldom telling Watson what he is up to, Jeeves often working behind Bertie's back; the dénouement; the company fawning on Holmes or Jeeves; the return trip to 'the rooms' in town; possibly Holmes's '...and I pocket my fee' paralleled by Bertie Wooster's 'How much money is there on the dressing-table, Jeeves? ... Collar it all. You've earned it!'"

In another, nonliterary field Doyle had an impact on Wodehouse--that of spiritualism, of which in his last decade Sir Arthur was the world's most dogged crusader. Between 1923 and 1925 Wodehouse attended at least three séances, Phelps reports, declaring in a letter from this period that spiritualism was "the goods." In 1965 he told a reporter that he had no fear of dying because "I'm a Spiritualist, like my friend Conan Doyle." At his death his library contained 62 books on spiritualism and related subjects. Despite such flirtation, however, Wodehouse had too much common sense to be taken in like his mentor. His grandson, Edward Cazalet, in a personal communication, says, "I have no doubt whatsoever that ultimately he had wholly rejected spiritualism as having any actual significance, and indeed any significance so far as he was concerned." As for the Anglican (Episcopal) faith in which he was baptized, his grandson, who visited him, on average, every other year from about 1955 until his death, never knew his grandfather to attend church, even at Easter or Christmas. When Malcolm Muggeridge asked him in the course of a BBC TV interview whether he believed in the hereafter, he paused for a few moments and then simply replied, "I'll wait and see."

Like Holmes a materialist, Lovecraft had no more use for spiritualism than he did for organized religion. Myths and imaginative stories were more to his youthful taste. In a letter dating to 1916 he cited Poe as his "God of Fiction," though Doyle held an honored place in his literary pantheon as well: "I used to write detective stories very often, the works of A. Conan Doyle being my model so far as plot was concerned." A wee tot when the initial series of adventures appeared in the *Strand,* he was fortuitously just the right age, as he wrote to a friend in 1918, when the stories later collected in *The Return* began their magazine run: "As for 'Sherlock Holmes'--I used to be infatuated with him! I read every Sherlock Holmes story published, and even organised my own detective agency when I was thirteen, arrogating to myself the proud pseudonym of S.H."

As a boy Lovecraft was an avid chemist, his grandfather fixing up a laboratory for him in the family basement. As a teenager, in an abortive effort to gain some professional training, he took a chemistry course through correspondence. In "Cool Air" Hector Muñoz has a laboratory in his New York apartment; Charles Dexter Ward establishes one in his London rooms. Alarmingly enough, as in Baker Street we hear of no source of running water readily at hand, an absolute necessity for anyone experimenting with chemicals, even an amateur working in the home.

As Martin J. Swanson has shown in his *Baker Street Journal* article, "Sherlock Holmes and H. P. Lovecraft" (1964), there are traces of Doyle in the weird-tale author, though these are truly traces compared to those in Wodehouse. The description of backwoods New England in "The Picture in the House," for example, parallels Holmes's ruminations on the remote English countryside in "The Adventure of the Copper Beeches." The Lovecraft story that comes closest to following the Holmes formula, "The Thing on the Doorstep," features a Watson-like narrator, Daniel Upton, whose stolidity contrasts sharply with the eccentricity of his precocious and daring friend, Edward Derby. "The Unnamable" contains a passing reference to Doyle, as philosopher if not creator of Sherlock Holmes.

For all his obscurity, Lovecraft did share a link with Doyle through Harry Houdini, meeting the celebrated magician and escape artist more than once on revision business. While Lovecraft dismissed Houdini as a "clever showman" and

P. G. Wodehouse
A. Conan Doyle
and H. P. Lovecraft
ca. 1903

pointed up his vanity in the ghostwritten tale "Under the Pyramids," they were united in their opposition to spiritualism. As Houdini relates in his book *A Magician Among the Spirits* (1924), he had a falling out in 1922 with his friend Sir Arthur after a spirit-writing séance conducted by Lady Doyle. Houdini took offense when Lady Doyle purported to transmit a message from his late, sainted mother in English, a language she spoke at best brokenly and never learned to write. Before the magician's untimely death in 1926 put an end to the project, Lovecraft wrote an outline of an antispiritualist book, provisionally titled "The Cancer of Superstition."

"H. P. G. WODECRAFT"

Neil Gaiman has claimed, with tongue in cheek, that he possesses the correspondence between Wodehouse and Lovecraft, as well as fragments of their musical, *Necronomicon Summer*, which includes a song with the refrain "I'm just a fool who / Thought that Cthulhu / Could fall in love!" In truth, it is unlikely that either man was familiar with, let alone appreciated, the other's work. Wodehouse was widely read, but I doubt that he even heard of Lovecraft, unless he caught Edmund Wilson's scathing *New Yorker* notice. Having no taste for horror fiction, Wodehouse at least might have liked the early Dunsanian fantasies had he read them. (In his autobiographical *Performing Flea*, he says of Lord Dunsany, "He is the only writer I know who opens up an entirely new world to me. What a mass of perfectly wonderful stuff he has done.") Lovecraft must have known Wodehouse by name, but in all the millions of words in the thousands of extant letters covering hundreds of literary subjects there is no mention whatsoever of Jeeves and Wooster.

In any event, two authors more disparate in style and substance, not to mention attitude toward life, would be hard to imagine. Wodehouse, for instance, relied heavily on dialogue, accustomed as he was to writing for the stage, notably lyrics for musicals. He turned a number of plays into novels and vice versa. Lovecraft, on the other hand, shunned dialogue, knowing he had no skill for it, as witness the labored exchanges in the closing pages of "The Dunwich Horror" and *The Case of Charles Dexter Ward*. No one could ever confuse a typical Wodehouse passage, full of witty word play, with a typical Lovecraft specimen, full of cosmic portentousness. Yet the two are not without certain affinities.

During his second American sojourn, Wodehouse contributed to the pulp magazines, observing in *Over Seventy* that in New York in 1909 there was "practically one per person." (In 1931 HPL echoed this sentiment, remarking in a letter on the proliferation of specialized fiction magazines: "I wouldn't be the least surprised to see *Undertaking Stories* or *True Plumber's Tales*--to say nothing of *Garbage-Collecting Adventures* & *Real Newsboy Mysteries*--on the stands any day.") One evening in 1914 Wodehouse dined with the editor of a string of pulps to whom he sold stories, Robert H. Davis, who in 1923 would reject "The Rats in the Walls" because, according to Lovecraft, it was "too horrible." In *Over Seventy* Wodehouse also notes, "If it had not been for the pulps--God bless them--I should soon have been looking like a famine victim." He later found a steady market in the higher paying, slick magazines, like the *Saturday Evening Post*, while Lovecraft limited himself to the pulps, chiefly *Weird Tales*. Subsisting in his last years on a frugal and unbalanced diet, HPL often struck those who knew him as resembling a famine victim.

In *The Dream-Quest of Unknown Kadath,* King Kuranes, "Lord of Ooth-Nargai," can be as petulant as Wodehouse's Lord Emsworth, "wishing that his old nurse would come in and scold him because he was not ready for that hateful lawn-party at the vicar's." While humor, other than in this fantasy novel, is all but absent from Lovecraft's fiction, it helps humanize his letters. Like Wodehouse, he realized the comic potential of language, in particular the amusing contrast between high and low speech. In person Lovecraft tended to sound like Jeeves, formal and Augustan, though he was just as adept at the sort of jaunty slang favored by Bertie. According to his friend James Morton, "He was probably the only twentieth century person in either England or America who actually talked, without the faintest effort or affectation, after the manner of Dr. Samuel Johnson, and followed the same practice in his letters. There was no posing in this, which was to him an absolutely natural mode of expression. In his light moments, he delighted in playfully indulging himself in modern slang, and thus going to the opposite pole from his normal method; and when he did so, he did it well and showed complete mastery of his linguistic material." Such suggests that Lovecraft might have produced comedy worthy of Wodehouse had he set his mind to it.

Lovecraft's personal life, for that matter, was at times the stuff of Wodehousian comedy. Like Bertie Wooster, he was devoted to his aunts, who helped raise him and were his only close family after his mother's death in 1921. Having no regular job, he could spend hours hanging around with his pals, themselves a mixture of bohemians and idlers--at least during his New York years from 1924 to 1926, when he was at his most sociable. His endless whinings about proper clothes in his voluminous letters to his Aunt Annie Gamwell make him sound like a penniless version of the sartorially conscious Bertie Wooster, author of that knowing article, "What the Well-dressed Young Man is Wearing." Adhering to a gentlemanly code, he was loyal to friends, chivalrous to ladies, and kind to cats. He politely answered every fan letter, such scrupulousness often leading to extensive epistolary exchanges, especially with aspiring young horror writers, whose immature efforts he would gladly offer to edit or even revise for free.

Unlike Sherlock Holmes, who was wise enough to avoid getting romantically entangled with Irene Adler, *the* woman "of dubious and questionable memory," Lovecraft plunged into marriage with disastrous results. It was his misfortune, perhaps, not to have a Jeeves figure to consult before deciding to elope--which HPL did almost as impulsively as Bertie whenever he got engaged. In this one instance Lovecraft treated a lady, his wife, less than chivalrously, rather shabbily in fact, fleeing back to his aunts in his native Providence, where he was content to resume, as he put it in a letter, "a dour celibate dignity." In *Lovecraft: A Biography* (1975), L. Sprague de Camp supplies the gory details. Suffice it to say here that he was not cut out to be either an ardent lover or a reliable breadwinner. As Jeeves said of Bertie, he was one of nature's bachelors.

Finally, like Bertie and his chums, Lovecraft had a penchant for assigning his friends funny nicknames, such as "Klarkash-Ton" for Clark Ashton Smith, "Melmoth the Wandrei" for Donald Wandrei, "Hilly Billy" Crawford for William L. Crawford, and "Sonny" or "Kid" or "Belknapius" for Frank Belknap Long, Jr. I rest my case.

DEAD WHITE EUROPEAN MALES

Doyle, Wodehouse, and Lovecraft, to begin by stating the obvious, share a common Anglo-Saxon heritage, notwithstanding Doyle's Irish ancestry. No matter that Lovecraft is American and the other two British, given the former's rabid Anglo-philism and the latters' fondness for the United States. American characters abound in the Sherlock Holmes stories, notably *A Study in Scarlet* and *The Valley of Fear* with their long (and tedious) subplots set in the U.S.A. In "The Adventure of the Noble Bachelor," the detective warmly refers to "citizens of the same world-wide country under a flag which shall be a quartering of the Union Jack with the Stars and Stripes." Americans parade through the works of Wodehouse, who often crossed the Atlantic, spending the last two decades of his long life on Long Island, where he died a dual British-U.S. citizen, shortly after receiving his long-awaited knighthood. Lovecraft, who affected English spelling and proudly pointed to his colonial New England roots, once vowed that if ever he could afford to travel there he would never leave old England. Perhaps his finest single tale, "The Rats in the Walls," concerns an American who claims an ancient family estate in England.

Given their genteel Victorian upbringings, they cannot avoid reflecting certain attitudes and biases peculiar to their class and culture. Servants, for example, figure in the work of all three authors. As a valet or "gentleman's gentleman," Jeeves shares equal billing with his master, Bertie Wooster. Many of Holmes's clients belong to the servant class, as of course does his landlady, Mrs. Hudson, who from time to time performs him services beyond the call of ordinary domestic duty. Servants never rise to the forefront in Lovecraft, yet they do appear on occasion, from the hapless victims in "From Beyond" to the "incredibly aged couple" and "swarthy young wench" in "The Thing on the Doorstep." As for valets, de la Poer dispenses with one, as usual, at bedtime in "The Rats in the Walls," while Randolph Carter employs a Cockney "man" in "The Silver Key." When in *The Dream-Quest* Carter calls on Kuranes, who dwells in "a grey Gothic manor-house" near an ersatz Cornish fishing village, he is met at the door by "a whiskered butler in suitable livery." In "Facts Concerning the Late Arthur Jermyn and His Family," "aged Soames," the family butler, provides the most trustworthy account of Arthur Jermyn's demise. In *The Case of Charles Dexter Ward*, the senior Wards' butler, a "worthy Yorkshireman," sends in his notice when the young master gives him a nasty look. No doubt in the circumstances Jeeves would have done the same.

Higher up the social scale, those with the means to employ servants tend to be well educated at a time when only an elite few had the benefit of a university education, either in Britain or America. (After graduation from public, i.e. private, school, Wodehouse joined a bank; his parents didn't have the money to send him to Oxford. Lovecraft dropped out of high school for health reasons; he always rued not being a university man.) Holmes went to university, though whether Oxford or Cambridge remains a matter of debate. After Eton Bertie Wooster attended Oxford, where Arthur Jermyn took "highest honours." Professors on the faculty of Arkham's Miskatonic University act as protagonists in several major Lovecraft tales. After a "none too brilliant graduation from the Moses Brown School," a private boys school in Providence, Charles Ward makes "positive his refusal to attend college." To his parents' disappointment, their nerdy son elects instead to pursue his arcane researches, first at home and later abroad.

Conspicuously missing from the list of young Ward's activities at Moses Brown is any mention of sports. In this lack his chronicler reflects Lovecraft's own distaste for games, whether physical like football or mental like chess. (Walking to exhaustion was about the only exercise HPL enjoyed.) In contrast, Doyle and Wodehouse, both tall, large, athletic men, relished games, including boxing, as their fiction shows. In "The Adventure of the Solitary Cyclist" Holmes, a skilled pugilist, modestly says, "I have some proficiency in the good old British sport of boxing." (Doyle himself excelled as an amateur heavyweight.) The boxer Battling Billson plays a featured role in a couple of Wodehouse's Ukridge stories. If boxing does figure in three of Lovecraft's earlier tales, the contests therein scarcely do this most manly of sports credit. An "exceedingly clever boxing match" between Alfred Jermyn and a circus gorilla goes fatally array in "Facts Concerning the Late Arthur Jermyn and His Family"; likewise Buck Robinson, "The Harlem Smoke," is knocked out permanently in one of the "Herbert West" episodes; finally, "a nocturnal fist fight atop the Great Pyramid" proves to be a "frame-up" that lures Houdini to his near doom in "Under the Pyramids."

Although their admirers might wish it otherwise, none of the three can escape the charge of racism in their fiction, especially against blacks. Doyle, a fair-minded man who often championed the underdog regardless of color, comes off as the least racist, the canon containing only one African-American caricature, the "savage" Steve Dixie in "The Adventure of the Three Gables." Dixie arrives at Baker Street to deliver a threat, though is deferential enough to address the detective as "Masser Holmes." He cuts an almost comic figure, wearing "a very loud gray check suit with a flowing salmon-coloured tie." (Besides being a bully and a coward, he dresses in poor taste.) More deserving of our pity than our fear, Dixie is still a human being-- which is more than the narrator of "Herbert West: Reanimator" will allow for Buck Robinson, "a loathsome, gorilla-like thing, with abnormally long arms which I could not help calling fore legs." A kinder if no less demeaning image of negroes appears in *The Case of Charles Dexter Ward* in the form of "old Asa and his stout wife Hannah," who let Ward inspect their home that in grander days once housed his ancestor. Then there is the notorious "Nigger-Man," the black cat named after an actual boyhood pet, in "The Rats in the Walls." As Lovecraft's letters reveal, even in his last years after he became more tolerant of Jews and other minorities, he remained convinced, sad to say, that blacks were barely above apes on the evolutionary ladder.

In some respects Wodehouse offers the most embarrassing examples of racial stereotyping. In a key plot twist in the first Jeeves novel, *Thank You, Jeeves*, Bertie disguises himself in blackface in an effort to pass as a "nigger minstrel." In "Jeeves and the Chump Cyril," set in New York, Jeeves passes on Bertie's bright purple socks of which he disapproves to an elevator operator, who is much obliged to "Misto' Jeeves." Here a "coloured chappie," in Bertie's phrase, besides having like Steve Dixie a weakness for flashy clothes, knows his place well enough to defer to a white valet. (In its original form, as a chapter in *The Inimitable Jeeves*, this story was titled "Startling Dressiness of a Lift Attendant.")

In *The Mating Season*, as an example of "a knockabout cross-talk act," Bertie describes that staple of traditional English music-hall comedy, a Pat and Mike routine (i.e., two dim Irishmen swap bad jokes and blows). As recently as 1957 Wodehouse could jest in *Over Seventy* about there being too many pigeons in New York, just as there are "far too many Puerto Ricans." (This comment doesn't appear in the U.S. edition, entitled *America, I Like You*, which differs substantially from the British.) In our own time English comedians would seem to assume mainstream audiences find ethnic humor more acceptable than their American counterparts. Think of the bumbling Spanish waiter in John Cleese's 1970s TV series "Fawlty Towers." "Don't mind him, he's from Barcelona," quips Basil, the irate innkeeper, whenever Manuel does anything especially dumb. (A generation ago American television could get away with portraying an ethnic-slur spouting Archie Bunker because he was stupid.)

To date none of Wodehouse's biographers has addressed his bigotry, as for example L. Sprague de Camp did Lovecraft's at such painful length. On the other hand, Lovecraft was a kind of misfit, in his darker moods a misanthrope, whereas the ever cheery Wodehouse was a genial, generous-hearted chap, with scarcely a harsh word for anyone, even in the privacy of his letters. This is the man, after all, Owen Dudley Edwards tells us, for whose soul a priest agreed to pray, with the qualification "in the case of someone who brought such joy to so many people in the course of his life, do you think it's necessary?" Even to raise the race issue in regard to Wodehouse seems churlish. Nonetheless, all sensitive readers of *Thank You, Jeeves* must wince every time Bertie Wooster, "mentally negligible" though he may be, uses the word *nigger*. (As a rule Europeans fail to recognize, even today, how pejorative this epithet is.) Alas, Wodehouse, like Doyle and Lovecraft, could not help harboring the racial prejudices held by most persons of noncolor before our own more enlightened, multicultural age.

AUDIENCE RESPONSE

In "Satisfaction" (1989), his *New Yorker* appreciation of the omnibus *World of Jeeves*, Terrence Rafferty points out, "The problem with Wodehouse is that his fiction, for all its aggressive frivolity, is manifestly the work of a genius: it compels our attention and affection the way great literature is supposed to." Anthony Quinton presents this problem another way when he says in "P. G. Wodehouse and the Comic Tradition," his introduction to Eileen McIlvaine's *P. G. Wodehouse: A Comprehensive Bibliography and Checklist* (1990), "For the most part critics do not know quite what to make of Wodehouse." By critics I suspect Quinton means those in professional or academic circles, many of whom tend to take a dry if not downright humorless approach to literature. Tellingly, Kristin Thompson could interest neither a university press nor a commercial house in her brilliant scholarly study, *Wooster Proposes, Jeeves Disposes* (1992), which came out under the imprint of James H. Heineman, a book publisher specializing in Wodehouse.

The situation is a little better for Doyle and Lovecraft. Bobbs-Merrill issued Samuel Rosenberg's Freudian interpretation of the canon, *Naked Is the Best Disguise* (1974), with success; while the renowned semiotician Umberto Eco in collaboration with others produced *The Sign of Three* (1983). Lovecraft has achieved a certain respectability as a subject for academic discourse, as represented by *Four Decades of Criticism* (1980), from Ohio University Press, and *An Epicure in the Terrible* (1991), an anthology of centennial essays published by Fairleigh Dickinson University Press. Still and all, as with Wodehouse, they are apt to compel the attention and affection not of English professors but of amateur scholars, who typically circulate their findings only among a small core of fellow enthusiasts.

Since Ronald Knox set the tone for all later Higher Criticism of the Sacred Writings in his seminal "Studies in the Literature of Sherlock Holmes" (1912), there has been a vast flow of secondary works, ranging from "biographies" like Vincent Starrett's classic *Private Life* (1933) and William S. Baring-Gould's sentimental *Sherlock Holmes of Baker Street* (1962) to specialized studies like Nicholas Utechin's *Sherlock Holmes at Oxford* (1981) and Christopher Redmond's *In Bed with Sherlock Holmes* (1984). Early on students of the canon took as a cardinal rule of the game that Holmes and Watson actually existed, that Doyle was at most Watson's literary agent. Hence all the awkward attempts to reconcile the chronology of the canon, an ultimately fruitless exercise because Doyle did not bother about consistency. Some commentators of late have bucked this trend, turning to Sir Arthur's life to explicate the fiction, like Owen Dudley Edwards in *The Quest for Sherlock Holmes* (1983).

A similar secondary literature exists for Wodehouse, though it is far less extensive. Again, many assume his characters were real. In *Thank You, Wodehouse* (1981), J.H.C. Morris examines such matters as Bertie's age, college at Oxford, make of car, and drinking habits. By sticking to the known facts, as it were, Morris nicely does for Wodehouse's world what Starrett did for Sherlock Holmes. Then there is C. Northcote Parkinson's biography, *Jeeves* (1979), which speculates beyond the known in such a delightfully droll way that no purist could object. Though there have been attempts to set an order and time span for the stories and novels in the Jeeves/Wooster series, a host of temporal contradictions doom all such efforts, as Kristin Thompson has shown in an appendix to her opus. N.T.P. Murphy, author of *In Search of Blandings* (1986), has discovered many place sources, but on the whole Wodehouse's fiction, with its dearth of dates and sparse topical references, does not lend itself to the sort of detailed annotation that Baring-Gould has done for Sherlock Holmes or Joshi is presently doing for Lovecraft.

His fans play something of the same game with Lovecraft, to assume that the various gods and forbidden books, notably the *Necronomicon*, are real. Fritz Leiber did it most poignantly in his tribute, "To Arkham and the Stars." One can construct a chronology for our own human era (HPL supplies plenty of dates in his fiction), as well as a sequence for the entire cosmos based, in particular, on *At the Mountains of Madness* and "The Shadow Out of Time." Lovecraft's cosmic history, however, has its gaps and inconsistencies. August Derleth, founder of Arkham House and popularizer of the term "Cthulhu Mythos," was the first disciple to impose a system on the master's tales, believing he was on the true path when he propounded his pantheon of the "Old Ones." Later devotees, like Richard Tierney and Dirk Mosig, have since refuted Derleth. In Lovecraft's case, being too precise can spoil the magic. Robert M. Price's Mythos family tree, diagrammed in the Hallowmas 1993 issue of *Crypt of Cthulhu,* shows how elaborate the game can get. If this sort of activity borders on the tiresome, it should be noted that Lovecraft himself liked to indulge in it, especially in his correspondence.

For his most ardent fans, however, it is less Lovecraft's imaginative inventions than the man himself who inspires their love. After all, his tales provide no fully developed, let alone endearing characters. Where is his Holmes or his Watson, his Jeeves or his Wooster? Upton and Derby are but shadows, like many of his characters of interest largely as projections of himself. Fortunately, as Vincent Starrett put it, Lovecraft was "his own most fantastic creation." From the five Arkham House volumes of letters, as well as from the letter collections to individual correspondents now being issued by Necronomicon Press, emerges a figure as fascinating as Sherlock Holmes. As an epistolarian, Lovecraft far outshines either Wodehouse or Doyle (or just about anyone else living in this century). It is perhaps another sign of the power of his personality that others have used him as a fictional character, like Richard Lupoff in his novel *Lovecraft's Book* and Fred Chappell in his story "Weird Tales."

Of course, another, more usual form of reverence is outright imitation, as well as pastiche and parody. Lovecraft encouraged his friends to add to his artificial mythology in their own work, and since his death there has been a slew of "Cthulhu Mythos" tales, though few of a quality equal to the originals. The stories that do Lovecraft most justice, like T.E.D. Klein's "Black Man with a Horn" and Fred Chappell's "The Adder," do so because their authors ring fresh changes in literate prose, eschewing formula clichés. Most Mythos fictioneers have been youthful novices, who at best may move on to develop a distinctive style of their own, like Ramsey Campbell, or to achieve a level of commercial competence, like Brian Lumley.

In the case of Conan Doyle, who was perfectly content to let others borrow Sherlock Holmes, a steady stream of imitations began almost immediately, as Paul D. Herbert outlines in his survey, *The Sincerest Form of Flattery* (1983). Early examples range from Mark Twain's sour satire, "A Double-Barrelled Detective Story," to A. B. Cox's parody-pastiche, "Holmes and the Dasher," in the manner of P. G. Wodehouse. The stream turned into a flood after 1974, the year of Nicholas Meyer's best-selling *The Seven-Per-Cent Solution*, in which Holmes between Reichenbach and his resurrection consults Sigmund Freud in Vienna. While the novel cleverly accounts for a number of loose ends, such as how the detective overcame his cocaine habit, the purists were distressed to see their hero reduced to a weak, all-too-human psychological study. In 1978 they had even greater cause for dismay when Michael Dibdin had the gall in *The Last Sherlock Holmes Story* to reveal the detective, in graphic detail, as Jack the Ripper! This was not playing the game like a gentleman. Since then, in the United States, all such pastiches must be first approved by the Doyle estate. Purists, too, have produced their share of novels teaming up

Holmes with this or that fictional or historical personage, from Dracula and Fu Manchu to Oscar Wilde and Harry Houdini. Michael Hardwick in *Prisoner of the Devil*, for example, has Holmes travel to Devil's Island to interview Alfred Dreyfus. For many fans rereading the 60 canonical adventures, clearly, is simply not enough.

If Wodehouse has not prompted imitation on nearly the same scale, it is at least in part because he wrote so much, almost a hundred books. With 11 novels in the Jeeves cycle, who needs a twelfth? But beyond this, anyone with the audacity to mimic the master faces the daunting task of trying to capture his style. As Terrence Rafferty says in his review, "These stories are, above all, a nearly exhaustive series in the comic possibilities of language." One needs to be almost as much of a genius with words as Wodehouse himself to pull off the trick. According to Richard Usborne, "A great number of people have tried to parody the 'Bertie Wodehouse' style in print. Rather fewer have tried to imitate it without parody. None has succeeded." In my view, one author of late has succeeded, though without resorting to either parody or imitation. In two novels, *Blue Heaven* and *Putting on the Ritz*, and one short story, "Great Lengths," Joe Keenan has updated and adapted the Bertie-Jeeves formula to contemporary New York society. He has devised plots as complex--and hilarious--as any in Wodehouse, employing a metaphoric style that rivals his predecessor's. Keenan's narrator and his chums may be openly and unashamedly homosexual, yet their world is also an innocent one, free of such unpleasant realities as gay-bashing and AIDS. Those amused by Jeremy Brett's campy portrayal in the most recent and most faithful TV adaptations of the adventures will find nothing offensive in Keenan.

Since the 1930s, when Christopher Morley and his buddies banded together in an all-male club, setting the pattern for other, scion societies worldwide, the Baker Street Irregulars have held an annual dinner in New York, around the time of Holmes's birthday in early January. In the late 1970s, acolytes of "Plum," as he was known to his friends (as a child he had trouble pronouncing "Pelham"), formed the Wodehouse Society, which publishes a quarterly newsletter called *Plum Lines* and gathers every two years for a weekend of jollity. The New York-based Drones, a dozen or so loyal Wodehousians, "meet for three dinners a year, and possibly a luncheon about Christmas time." No formal Lovecraft society has ever gotten off the ground, though his fans frequently assemble at horror or fantasy conventions, keeping in touch through amateur press associations and the mail. In New York the "New Kalems" meet regularly at coffee shops, Irish taverns, and bookstores, to enjoy the kind of low-cost camaraderie that the Kalems of old did, to engage in the sort of good-natured and boyish banter that might lead a stranger overhearing their conversation to agree with Edmund Wilson when he sniffed: "But the Lovecraft cult, I fear, is on even a more infantile level than the Baker Street Irregulars and the cult of Sherlock Holmes."

P. H. CANNON has contributed articles to such journals as the *Baker Street Journal*, *Plum Lines*, and *Lovecraft Studies*. He has been known to attend official gatherings of the Baker Street Irregulars and of the Wodehouse Society, as well as to hang out with the New Kalems in New York City.

J. C. ECKHARDT has been to London, seen seven wonders, including the Lost Sea and the Pyramid of the Moon. His presence has been tolerated for a long time among the Providence Pals, and his artwork has been seen in such diverse places as *Twilight Zone Magazine*, Necronomicon Press, T-shirts, and the Newport (R.I.) Art Club